By J.L. O'FAOLAIN

NOVELS

NO MORE HEROES SERIES
Push Comes to Shove
Scratch & Sniff
Wrath & Ruin

SECTION THIRTEEN STORIES
The Thirteenth Child
The Thirteenth Pillar
The Thirteenth Sigil
The Thirteenth Shard

Published by DREAMSPINNER PRESS
http://www.dreamspinnerpress.com

WRATH & RUIN

J.L. O'Faolain

Dreamspinner Press

Published by
Dreamspinner Press
5032 Capital Circle SW
Suite 2, PMB# 279
Tallahassee, FL 32305-7886
USA
http://www.dreamspinnerpress.com/

Wrath & Ruin
© 2013 J.L. O'Faolain.

Cover Art
© 2013 Paul Richmond.
http://www.paulrichmondstudio.com
Cover content is for illustrative purposes only and any person depicted on the cover is a model.

ISBN: 978-1-62798-240-5
Digital ISBN: 978-1-62798-239-9

Printed in the United States of America
First Edition
December 2013

To my birth father.
Rest in peace, Papa.

ACKNOWLEDGMENTS

To the Lord and Lady; to my wonderful Internet family and the family I've built in real life; to Caty, for giving me such a splendid vacation.

And to all of you.

Thank you.

PROLOGUE

THE HOUSE was quiet.

For once, fortune seemed to be in Wrath's favor as he slid the back door shut. Remembering that Scarlet Queen and Wiccan Witch were camped out in the living room, he eschewed flipping on a light switch. A candlewick-sized puff of flame appeared in the palm of his hand instead as he stepped forward through the back foyer. Wrath closed his fingers around the fire to block some of the light as he passed through the living room.

His bedroom was just inside the hall to his right. Seeing no movement from the two futons on the floor, Wrath slipped noiselessly into his room and shut the door behind him. Once there, the flame in his hand automatically went out. Wrath switched on the light and sat down, placing the package he'd been carrying on the bed next to him.

For a minute he remained perfectly still, staring down at the metal box.

"Come in," he called out to Wiccan Witch, who he sensed was standing on the other side of the door.

A second later, the door popped open. There stood Wiccan Witch, one hand still raised in a fist like she was about to knock.

"Empath, remember?" he said.

"That's pretty damn cool," she said, smiling at him. "Sorry if I was disturbing you. I'd gotten up to use the bathroom and saw your light on."

"You wanted to see if I was planning on murdering everyone while they slept?"

Wrath frowned slightly when Wiccan Witch didn't flinch at the remark. "You don't fit the profile of a compulsive killer," she retorted. "For one thing, there haven't been any pets reported missing since you guys showed up."

"It's still early," Wrath said, raising an eyebrow in challenge. "And between the plane crash and giant robots, going after cute puppy dogs wouldn't get me nearly the amount of attention I crave."

Wiccan Witch's smile didn't fade. If anything, it grew broader.

"Forgive my annoying tendency to be nosy, but what's that?" she asked, pointing to the box on the bed. "Is that what you were looking for?"

The comment startled Wrath.

"I was there when the sheriff mentioned it," she pointed out, "remember?"

Wrath did and kicked himself silently for not putting the box in the spacious closet just a few feet away when he first walked in.

"It's something I lost back when I was here before," he told her, sensing she wanted to sit down. "When I came back the first time and was caught."

Wrath moved over some, even though there was plenty of room. Wiccan Witch accepted the invitation, however, and surprised him by sitting down between him and the box.

"Do you mind?" she asked, reaching for it.

Wrath shrugged, pretending it didn't matter, but watched closely as Wiccan Witch held the metal container up gingerly with both hands.

"It looks old," she noted. "Banged up, too."

"It was inside an old storehouse," he explained. "One of those places where the local police keep old evidence. I'd been going through the town records since I got here trying to find it."

Wiccan Witch's hand brushed up against the small lock holding the box closed. "Here," she said, passing it to Wrath. "It's yours. You should be doing this instead of me."

Wrath took the box from her, then went digging into a pants pocket for a pair of wire clippers. "The lock's been on there for ages," he said. "It doesn't look like anyone tried to open it after I was arrested."

Wrath held the lock between the wire cutter's teeth. "The key wasn't where I remember hiding it before I ran away," he went on, waiting a moment before breaking the lock. "It must have been thrown away when the house was renovated."

Wiccan Witch was watching him closely. "Do you need me to go?" she asked plainly. "I don't mind if you want to be alone for this."

Wrath considered her offer for a moment. "No," he decided, hair falling into his face as he shook his head. "You can stay."

Wiccan Witch smiled and brushed the stray locks out of Wrath's face so he could see what he was doing. Grasping the cutter tightly, he gave a soft grunt of satisfaction as the tool snapped the lock right off.

Wiccan Witch reached over and plucked the broken lock off Wrath's leg for him while he thumbed the latch open.

"You're right," she said, noting the latch's resistance toward being moved. "It doesn't look like this thing's been opened in years. I guess that means whatever is inside hasn't been tampered with."

"Good to know," Wrath said before slowly raising the lid. "I'd hate to have to hurt someone over this just when I was getting used to the idea of being a good guy."

A smile tugged at Wiccan Witch's mouth, but she held her laughter in while Wrath opened the metal box. Now that she thought about it, the box resembled an old container for tools.

Wrath's face, meanwhile, lit up as his hands touched whatever was inside.

"A comic book?"

Wrath turned the comic toward Wiccan Witch so she could read it. "Walt Disney Adventures?" she read aloud.

There were several other comics still inside. "Donald Duck," she read again, noting the title on the cover. "'Spider-Man, Storm, & Power Man Battle Smokescreen'?"

Wrath was blushing.

"It was one of those antismoking campaign things they pass out at school," he explained, covering the comic. "I got it in first grade."

Something else caught Wiccan Witch's eye. "What's that?" she asked, pointing at a small plastic lump in the shadows. "A toy truck?"

Wrath held the two-inch toy up for her to see. "It was the prize from a McDonald's Happy Meal," he said. "My mother hated eating out, but one day when we were in town, I managed to beg her into stopping at McDonald's. This was the prize they were giving away that day."

"And you kept it?"

The smile on Wrath's face faded a little. "I played with this thing for weeks," he said softly, "rolling it over furniture and the floor until she threatened to throw it away. I was so afraid I'd lose it. I stuck it under my bed near the headboard. Even then, I was convinced she'd find it, so I started looking for a better hiding place."

Wrath gazed down into the toolbox. "That's when I found this," he went on, touching the box's edges carefully. "It fell out of the back of my father's truck, and he didn't even notice. The lock and key were inside, so I snuck it into my room and started keeping things in it."

Something occurred to Wiccan Witch as she listened. "What about all your other stuff?" she asked, frowning. "Why did you keep these things?"

Wrath refused to look at her. "This was all of my stuff," he finally admitted, taking the truck out of her hand and putting it back in the box. "I was a bad kid. I wouldn't stop playing with matches and setting fire to things, so my parents punished me by giving away all my toys. I cried for the rest of the day when that happened."

Wrath's whole body went rigid as he realized what had just slipped from his mouth. "Anyway," he said in a terse voice, shutting the box with a loud snap. "After that, I hid anything that came my way in here so no one would steal it. At the time, it didn't dawn on me that I was making things easier by keeping it all in one convenient place."

"So you came back for it," Wiccan Witch said, understanding now. "After New Orleans, you came back to Shove Point to get it. That's what you were doing here."

Wrath scowled at her correct assumption. "Everything I'd had in New Orleans was gone," he muttered ruefully. "Losing all my toys the first time taught me that I had to cherish whatever came my way.

Eventually, it would be gone. When the Association brought down the Deadly Seven, I was back to square one. The only thing left to my name was what I'd neglected to take with me when Sloth made his offer, so I came back for it."

The room was dead quiet for several minutes. "I didn't want to be a criminal," he said, feeling foolish. "But I couldn't stay in Shove Point. They were talking about sending me away, and Sloth's offer was exciting. No one had ever treated what I could do like it was special or important. Thank Goddess I had Pride to look after me, or else I'd have died from doing some pretty stupid things."

"Have you heard from her?" Wiccan Witch asked warily, knowing Wrath might get the wrong idea. "Pride, I mean. Has she tried contacting you?"

Wrath glanced at her suspiciously for a moment, then relaxed. "No," he said. "The only members of the Deadly Seven I've had any contact with at all are the ones here in Shove Point, and them I could live without."

Wrath felt Wiccan Witch's eyes on him as he picked aimlessly through the box's contents. A small Ninja Turtle figure sat underneath a single issue of a He-Man comic. There was also a handful of change, some quarters and pennies scattered. Wrath couldn't remember what he'd done to earn that, or if he'd done anything at all. More than likely, it was change he'd picked up off the ground when no one was watching.

Slowly, Wrath closed the lid.

"I'm ready for my abuse now," he said dryly over the sound of the latch snapping back into place. "I know it was stupid, but it seemed important at the time."

Wrath jumped as he felt Wiccan Witch's hand slide over his. "It isn't stupid," she said, squeezing. "It's yours, so you should have it."

Wrath stayed perfectly still as Wiccan Witch waited patiently. "Don't tell anyone," he asked pleadingly, keeping his eyes forward. "I don't want anyone to know."

"I won't."

It was a bad idea. Wrath could think of a whole printout of reasons why he shouldn't do what they were about to do. When Wiccan

Witch slid the box out of his hands, he didn't try to stop her. Keeping both eyes on him, she leaned forward and slipped the box underneath the bed.

"I don't think anybody's going to check under there," she told him reassuringly.

Wrath looked at her finally, kicking himself the whole time. It was stupid, but he'd been in prison for a decade. Besides, there was an old proverb about how the bigger fool in a situation was the starving man who rejected an offer of free food.

Now that he'd decided that, though, there was the rather awkward matter of not knowing where to start. It had been a long time, and, despite his reputation, Wrath had never been the player most people assumed. Now, as Wiccan Witch grinned impishly at him, he wondered who the idiot was that started those rumors in the first place. All they'd done was set a bar impossibly high and leave him feeling inadequate next to his own reputation.

Wiccan Witch saved him the trouble by kissing him first. After that, things started to progress a little more smoothly. Pretty soon, Wrath was stretched out on top of the covers with his head against the pillow. Wiccan Witch's comfortable weight pressed him down into the mattress as they french kissed. Her body was soft in all the right places, but underneath that, Wrath's fingers touched the hard muscle built from a daily grind.

She was steel wrapped in silk and felt glorious. Her bangs tickled his forehead when she would tilt her head slightly. Wrath's senses were on overdrive as he forced himself to remember each miniscule detail. There was a chance this wouldn't happen a second time, so he was determined to recall everything.

Thinking this, his eyes flew open as her hand drifted down his shirt toward his pants.

"Not here," he said, jerking back far enough to speak.

Wiccan Witch blinked, startled by the sudden movement. "What?" she asked. "What's wrong?"

Wrath smirked sheepishly at her. "Oh, nothing like that," he reassured her. "It's just that... well, this used to be my parents' bedroom when I was a kid."

"Okay. And?"

A blush crept up his face as he met her eyes. "I've had enough trips down memory lane for one night," he tried feebly. "Is there any way we could do this somewhere else?"

The answer came to Wiccan Witch as she opened her mouth to ask why. "Oh," she said, pursing her lips. "I see."

Wrath shrugged, hoping it looked casual. "I think I was four," he elaborated. "It was before my powers started manifesting. I'd come to ask for a glass of water, and... things went downhill after that."

"Sucks to be them," Wiccan Witch retorted disdainfully. "But sure. Did you have a particular place in mind?"

Wrath thought quickly. "Scratch's room is probably free," he said. "I doubt he'll be using it anymore, and we could always wash the sheets for him."

Wiccan Witch laughed. "How thoughtful," she said teasingly.

Wrath shrugged again. "I'm evil," he stated, "but I'm not that cruel."

Wiccan Witch shot him a look that said she wasn't buying it. "I've got a better idea," she decided, getting up off him. "Is there a spare blanket or something around here?"

Wrath answered by getting off the bed after her and rolling up the heavy bedspread. "Done," he said, tossing it over one shoulder. "What now?"

"Come with me," she replied, taking him by the hand.

Wrath followed after her, remembering to kill the bedroom light on his way out. With Wiccan Witch in the lead, they eased quietly through the living room past Scarlet Queen, who was resting soundly on the futon.

"She's a light sleeper," Wiccan Witch warned. "Try not to bump into anything."

The moment those words left her lips, Wiccan Witch's toe struck the side of the couch. Wrath reacted fast, placing a hand over her mouth before she could cry out.

"Thanks," she said, after he pulled his hand away.

"No problem." Wrath tensed inside as the next sentence flew out before he could stop himself. "I know I'll regret asking, but is there a reason why we're sneaking around like a couple of teenagers?"

"Force of habit," she replied promptly. "My roommate has had problems sleeping through the night for years. The slightest noise will wake her up, so I have to creep around if I do anything in the middle of the night."

Wrath looked away, feeling bad now for asking.

"Come on," she said, taking his hand again. "Let's go."

Wiccan Witch led them out of the living room, into the kitchen, and through the foyer that connected Push's bedroom with the back door. Wrath kept his eyes facing forward, refusing to look back while Wiccan Witch fumbled with the lock. Closing the door behind them, he caught sight of Push's room before the back door blocked the view.

"Okay," he said, breathing in the cool night air. "What now?"

"This way."

A moment later, Wrath had spread the bedspread out onto the grass. Wiccan Witch had already disrobed and was helping him do the same.

"Are you sure?" he whispered in her ear as she kissed along his collarbone.

Wiccan Witch answered by seizing the back of his head and yanking him down. "Do it," she hissed out between kisses. "Please."

A decade behind prison walls had, if nothing else, given Wrath the time to expand on his diction.

"Okay."

Just as he felt the head of his shaft press against her soft folds, something flashed in the corner of Wrath's eye. Wiccan Witch saw it at the same time and jerked her head. Their eyes widened as three police cars came down the street in their direction with lights flashing.

"Shit!" Wrath swore, reaching for his pants.

Wiccan Witch was dressing herself at a speed that would have made Clark Kent feel proud. "What do they want?" she wondered, as Wrath stood with his pants on.

"Nothing good," he assured, standing close by, wearing a grim face. "I recognize that car. It's the sheriff."

CHAPTER
ONE

WARM.

He was so warm.

Push watched as Scratch's chest rose and fell in an easy rhythm. His best friend, his boyfriend, had been out like a light for hours. Push had dozed, meanwhile, waking every so often at the smallest sound. Each time, his eyes had drifted over Scratch, confirming the man entangled in his arms was real.

Feeling the solid weight of Scratch's body was pure bliss. Push tightened his hold on the man he loved, careful not to wake him, and savored each second that passed.

It had been a long day. In fact, it had been a long week for all of them. Push rewound the events in his head until they made him dizzy. So much had happened already. The worst part was that it wasn't over yet.

Something rattled behind him. Push turned toward the bedside table and saw his phone wobbling uncontrollably. He'd set it on vibrate before going to bed. For the past few days, the team had done little other than make phone calls. It was imperative that they account for each and every Real-Life Superhero Association member. A few stragglers still hadn't reported in yet.

After snatching the phone up, Push quickly untangled himself from Scratch, got out of bed, and dashed to the bathroom. Once inside, he flipped on the light switch and blinked spots out of his eyes before answering.

"Push?"

The voice made Push sigh in relief. "Mind Bender," he replied in answer, sitting down on the toilet. "Where the hell have you been?"

"In the hospital," Mind Bender said, and now Push could hear the noise on the other end of the line. It sounded as though Bender was still there.

"I've been visiting the people that were injured in the bombing," his friend continued. "The ones that made it out alive, at least. It's been a nightmare."

"I know," said Push, sighing heavily as the weight of the past forty-eight hours crashed down on his shoulders. "The team and I have spent most of our time tying up the phone lines, trying to account for who all is alive and who's dead."

"I just saw the latest update on the site," Bender said sadly. "They've found several more dead heroes in the rubble."

Push said nothing in reply.

"I was glad to see you and Scratch weren't there," Bender went on in a bittersweet tone. "Then I remembered that you were training the new guy somewhere down south."

"Right."

Push didn't know what else to say.

"How's that going?" Bender asked. "I heard he was a handful."

"Not really," Push admitted. "He hasn't been the real problem since the Cape Cabinet transferred us."

"What's been happening?"

Push let out a deep breath. "It's late," he said apologetically. "And a very long story."

"I'm waiting to hear whether Starbolt will live through the night," Bender replied gravely. "The medics pulled her out from under several warped support structures. Half of her rib cage is crushed, and she's probably damaged her spine. I'd rather hear a long story from you than sit in the waiting room not knowing whether to pray for her to live or to die in peace so she doesn't live the rest of her life as an invalid."

Push thought of the warm bed where Scratch was sleeping and the cold hospital waiting room that Mind Bender currently sat diligently in.

"Here goes," Push said before taking a deep breath. "You heard the part about Wrath, the new guy we're training, being an ex-con, right?"

"Right," Bender affirmed. "And that he's got a superpower like you."

"Not like me," Push corrected. "I'm telekinetic, as far as anyone can tell. Wrath has pyrokinesis. He starts and controls fires. Wrath was a member of the Deadly Seven."

Mind Bender stayed quiet for a second. "I was hoping that part was just office gossip," he said tersely. "What was the Cape Cabinet thinking?"

"Actually, he's not so bad," Push countered before he could stop himself. "Annoying, but nothing like I thought he'd be at first."

Mind Bender didn't sound completely convinced. "You remember what that guy has done, right?" he asked, keeping his tone neutral. "The guy isn't exactly the 'drink your milk, kids' type."

"No, he isn't," Push acknowledged. "And I know what he did when the Deadly Seven had the run of the New Orleans crime syndicate. Wrath doesn't deny any of that. I also learned why he joined the Seven in the first place."

Push paused to take a deep breath. "Much as I hate to admit it, that's made me look at him in a slightly different light. Plus, he's been a great big help down here since we arrived."

"It sounds as though you like the guy," Mind Bender teased. "Have you finally given up on crushing after your straight roommate? If Wrath isn't interested in guys, you might have some sort of complex going on."

Push winced on the inside. It had only come out a few days prior that several of his friends had known about Push's crush on Scratch all along. Apparently, the girth of that circle stretched farther than he'd thought.

"Funny," Push retorted, knowing he had the upper hand on Bender regardless. "I've wondered that same thing before. But no, I'm not pining for a former supervillain. Scratch and I have been too busy getting our own relationship off the ground for me to bother trying."

Nothing but the dim echo of waiting-room conversation came through the phone.

"Um. What?"

It was very hard for Push to keep from snickering. "Scratch and I are in a relationship now," he reiterated. "We got together not long after arriving in Shove Point."

More silence followed. "What?"

"Scratch is my boyfriend," Push clarified, unable to hold back the giggle fit he was having. "He's asleep in the next room right now. I could wake him up if you feel like you need to hear it from him."

Mind Bender was silent once more. "He doesn't mind if you know," Push went on, enjoying himself immensely. "In fact, Scratch was the one who brought up us telling all our friends so I didn't need to feel like it was some big secret."

It took Mind Bender a moment, but he finally found his voice. "Okay," he began, utterly befuddled. "Bizarro Push, would you mind giving the phone back to the man you were cloned from and stop messing with my head? Scratch is the biggest horndog in the whole Association. His tights see more action than Batman's."

"I can't speak for Batman," Push replied coolly. "But it's what Scratch has under the tights that impresses me."

Push snickered as Bender was stunned speechless yet again. "Talk to me about something else," Bender begged after a moment. "I need several minutes to process all this. Tell me about what's going on in the quiet, peaceful southern burb of Shove Point, Arkansas."

Push's mouth twisted into a frown. "The part about me and Scratch is actually the most normal thing happening right now."

"I refuse to believe that," Mind Bender insisted. "Talk, now."

"Well, a small commercial jet crash-landed on the town right after the Association made our transfer official," Push began.

"I heard about that," Bender said, his voice serious. "Until the Association building bombings, it sounded like the worst thing any of us have dealt with since the Big Brawl in New Orleans with the Deadly Seven."

"It was pretty bad," said Push. "The part where it gets weird was finding out that a spacecraft brought the plane down in the first place."

When Mind Bender said nothing, Push went on. "Then a bunch of aliens showed up late one night. They were snooping around in the rubble left by the plane like they were hunting for something. Wrath helped us track them through the woods to where the craft had washed up on the shore of a lake. Only it turned out that Wrath's old boss, Sloth, was looking for the damn thing too. We still haven't figured out what he wants with it, but Wrath was able to fight him off. Then the craft ejected a pod out of it and exploded."

"Uh," Bender began, but Push cut him off.

"We tried telling the Cape Cabinet what we found, but they've refused to comment. So we went back to capturing Sloth like they told us to. At least, that's what the plan was until our wheels came to life and went on a rampage. Apparently, someone stole a bunch of microbots that the organization's brain trust had been developing from an Association warehouse."

"Microbots?" Mind Bender interjected. "The Association is building microbots?"

"According to Professor Trixter, they are," Push said. "Someone stole them, though, and programmed the machines to go on a rampage through town. Luckily, Scarlet Queen, Wiccan Witch, and Trixter had come down for a visit. Even then, it wasn't easy. The microbots built giant bodies for themselves out of salvage-yard parts and almost stomped over the town."

"Giant robots," Bender said disbelievingly. "First spaceships, then aliens and microbots, and now giant robots crushing an already half-flattened town?"

"It's been a busy week," said Push, giving Bender a moment to absorb everything. "We got the giant robots shut down, but it was supposed to be temporary. Professor Trixter thinks that the machines will reactivate within the next twelve hours, give or take. It looks like tomorrow is going to be busy, and we still haven't captured Sloth."

Mind Bender was muttering to himself now. "Aliens," Push heard him whisper. "Spacecrafts, giant robots, and you and Scratch are dating now?"

"Yeah."

Before Push could finish answering, the line went dead. "Mind Bender?" Push asked, pressing the phone closer to his ear. "Hello?"

A dial tone followed.

"Weird," Push said, hitting the redial button.

All that followed was a busy signal. Concern gripped Push for a moment, but then he remembered that there had been no bombings reported anywhere other than Association property. "Maybe he got word about Starbolt," Push said out loud, getting up off the toilet. "Oh well."

Much as he hated dismissing an injured hero's plight, Push knew he would be no good to anyone if he didn't get some rest. There would be time tomorrow to mourn the fallen and check on how the recovering were doing.

The bed was calling to him, and so was the sleeping body resting comfortably inside it. Push couldn't help but smile when he caught sight of Scratch breathing deeply under the covers. Leaving the bathroom door open, he crossed the room and crawled in beside the man he loved.

Before Push closed his eyes, something Mind Bender had said popped into the forefront of his mind.

"It sounds as though you like the guy."

Mind Bender had some funny ideas. "I don't like Wrath," Push said to himself, tightening his hold on Scratch again. "Not that way, anyway. He's not so bad as a member of the Association, but...."

Whatever else Push had been about to say faded as sleep rolled over him. Just as his mind entered the threshold of what looked to be a wonderful dream, a loud knock jerked Push awake.

"What?" he shouted, rising up in shock and startling Scratch awake as well.

"Huh?" Scratch blinked and pushed himself up off his pillow as a sharp set of knocks echoed from the front of the house, followed by the doorbell.

"Who could that be?" Push wondered.

"No one with good news," Scratch replied calmly, rolling slowly out of bed. "No sane person would ever ring a doorbell at this hour."

The doorbell rang again, more insistent this time, and was punctuated by pounding. "I'm coming! I'm coming!" they heard Scarlet Queen shout from the living room. "The hell is wrong with you people?"

Push waited, listening as the living-room door swung open. Silence followed, only to be broken by the sound of an older man's voice speaking in a low but sharp tone. A moment later, Scarlet Queen's footsteps were heard stomping across the kitchen tile.

"We've got a problem," Scarlet Queen said as she entered Push's room unannounced.

"I'm not surprised," Push said, struggling into a pair of pants. "Who is it?"

"The sheriff," she answered flatly, leaning against the frame. "Apparently, we're all under arrest."

IT HADN'T been that long since they were inside the sheriff's department. Push had to remind himself of that as he and the others were led inside wearing handcuffs. Scarlet Queen, Wiccan Witch, and Professor Trixter hadn't been with them the first time they'd paid Black a visit after arriving at Shove Point. The same receptionist from before was sitting behind the glass window, watching them file in one after the other.

Inevitably, Sheriff Black had called his two favorite deputies, McGee and Fortenberry, to help load them up. Both men were grinning from ear to ear as though Christmas had come early.

"In here," Black said, directing them to the back where the row of cells was.

No one said a word. The others were behaving themselves for the moment, even Wrath. For some reason, the dark-haired man had been waiting outside with Wiccan Witch while Scarlet Queen woke Trixter up. Wrath and Wiccan Witch had been the first to get up and dressed, which struck Push as weird.

Push put the thought aside for now as he entered the jail cell behind Scratch. Black closed the cell door with a loud clank and locked it. The older man's eyes locked with Push's for a moment, when he turned back to give the sheriff a warning look. To his surprise, the sheriff didn't stick around to gloat. Black broke the gaze and marched off without a word.

"Anyone know exactly what it is we're in for?" Trixter wondered, getting Push's attention.

Wrath held up a hand and began listing things off. "Disturbing the peace," he began. "Destruction of private and public property, reckless endangerment, and failure to heed an officer of the law."

Everyone else but Push looked surprised. "It's my fault," he said, feeling tired and fed up. "Black sent us a message by way of one of his deputies after Duane, the Pranksta Gayngsta, tore up that pizza place. He wanted us out of town by the next morning. Because of the Association bombings, though, I forgot to report it to the lawyer division so they could take care of it."

"The lawyer division was hit too," Scratch reminded him. "It wouldn't have made any difference."

"Besides," Wiccan Witch added, glancing back and forth between Push, Professor Trixter, and Wrath for emphasis. "It isn't like any of us are actually trapped in here."

Wrath looked directly at Push. "I didn't think setting the cops on fire would have sat well with you," he said, and it just barely sounded like he was being apologetic. "Was I wrong?"

Push's mouth turned upward into a wry smile. "Not really," he replied begrudgingly. "We don't need to make the situation worse, but Black could not have chosen a worse possible time to pull something like this."

"Fuck," Scratch swore, looking thoroughly pissed. "It's not like we don't have enough on our plates as it is."

Scarlet Queen, who had been standing against the set of bars running perpendicular to the cell door, scowled for a moment and crossed both arms in front of her.

"What are we doing for the moment?" she asked, looking from one face to the next. "I mean, we're entitled to one phone call. They can't hold that against us."

"It'll probably be a while before the Association can send someone down here to get us out of this mess," Trixter pointed out, looking less than thrilled as well.

"So we wait?" Wiccan Witch asked patiently.

Push thought their options over for a moment, slowly forming a plan. "We may not have to," he decided, turning to the door at the end of the corridor the sheriff had left through. "Trixter, how much longer do you think it will be before those nanobots, or microbots, or whatever you want to call them, reactivate?"

Trixter's eyes widened a second before he pursed his lips in chagrin. "About that," he began, refusing to meet anyone's eyes. "Er, there's a small chance that they have already."

Scratch stared Trixter in the face and didn't turn away. "Um, how small of a chance are we talking here?"

Trixter stiffened. "Ninety-three percent," he answered sheepishly. "Give or take a tenth of a percent."

Trixter now had everyone's attention. "And you didn't think this was something we needed to know?" Wrath demanded.

Wiccan Witch held onto Wrath's arm, restraining him, but Wrath didn't back down. "Those things almost tore the town apart the first time," Wrath reminded Trixter as tiny sparks of flame danced between his fingertips. "I'd rather not be locked in here when they build new bodies and come looking for a rematch."

Trixter stared back at Wrath as though he was being scolded by a petulant child. "I said they would reactivate," Trixter reiterated. "That's not the same thing as them making new bodies for themselves right away."

"Not following," Scarlet Queen said.

Neither was anyone else from what Push could see. "The first time they went on a rampage," Trixter explained, "the nanobots—"

"Microbots," Scarlet Queen corrected. "They aren't small enough to fit the nano scale."

"Whatever," Trixter retorted, looking annoyed at her now. "The machines were new and untested. They were running amok, getting their feet wet. They took a beating from that electromagnetic pulse I fired out of the hovercraft. Then the town officials had those bodies the nanobots—"

"Microbots," Wrath corrected this time.

"Whatever," Push said gently.

"Those giant bodies burned," Trixter finished, waiting a moment to see if anyone else would interrupt. "The microbots can't snap back from something like that all at once. They'll reactivate, but it'll take some time before they can launch a full-scale assault like before. Assuming they're even programmed to do that. We still don't know why the traitor gave those to Sloth in the first place."

"To keep us distracted while Sloth located the pod," Wrath explained, as if the answer were obvious.

"There's probably more to it than that," Scratch said. "Um, who's to say those robots don't have more than one purpose?"

Judging by everyone's expression, no one wanted to think about that. "So either the microbots turn themselves back on and start remodeling the town," Push decided, "or the Association gets word that we're being held against our wills and sends someone to straighten this out."

"I don't want to stay long enough for the latter to happen," Wrath objected.

"None of us do," Scarlet Queen declared sourly before looking at Wrath. "Is everyone in this podunk town as petty as that sheriff?"

"Most of them," Wrath answered calmly. "It's a common Southern trait."

The news that Wrath had grown up in Shove Point appeared to be common knowledge among the group now. Push noticed that the others seemed a little more at ease around the man. When the Association buildings got bombed, Wrath had pitched in alongside everyone, doing whatever he could to help the team confirm which members across the nation were alive, dead, or injured. He'd also kept them well fed, stopping every so often to cook.

As a result, the group seemed to accept him more as one of their own. Wiccan Witch, above all others, looked especially pleased by his presence. Push chalked that up to them both following the same religious path, though a glint in the blonde woman's eyes as she looked over at Wrath made Push rethink that statement.

The cell had gotten quiet. Scratch shuffled over to his right, closer to Push. The movement startled Push, but then he relaxed and smiled as Scratch took hold of his hand. Feeling the weight of it there loosened the knot that had been forming in his chest, helping him relax. Scratch gave Push's hand a squeeze, which spread the warmth in his body through Push's hand, up his arm, and over the rest of his body.

Push looked up, a big goofy grin covering his face, and saw the whole cell was watching them.

Professor Trixter shook his head and chuckled. "You two have got it bad," he chided, giving them a smile of approval. "I hope it works out for you both."

Scratch looked at Push. "I'm not going anywhere," he said, squeezing Push's hand again a little harder than before.

It almost felt like Scratch was trying to anchor Push to his side. "Me either," Push said, hoping he sounded reassuring.

"Good."

There was that same tone as before, the one Scratch had used days ago when he'd acted like Push was going to get snatched up by some other man. The conversation with Mind Bender flashed through his mind. Push had to fight the urge to look at Wrath. Scratch was still facing him, and the last thing Push needed was to give his boyfriend the wrong idea.

That he'd rolled on top of Wrath and stayed there for longer than necessary during the fight with the transformed Duane.

That he'd watched the sweat roll down Wrath's body during their jog home.

Push tightened his own hold on Scratch's hand, as if in defiance. He'd loved Scratch for years, had convinced himself that nothing would come from pining for the man. Scratch considered himself straight, even though he said he loved Push. Push himself wasn't sure what to make of it or how their pieces fit together, but it didn't matter. He wanted to be with Scratch. He loved that Scratch loved him back.

Push let his eyes wander toward Wrath at last, who was still sitting quietly beside Wiccan Witch, their hands resting close to one another atop the bed.

This was how it should be, he insisted to himself.

It really was.

The loud crash from outside cut off any further attempts on Push's part to reassure himself. His friends sharing the cell jerked up at the same time, shaken out of whatever quiet thoughts they'd been having. Scratch had been watching Push closely, Push realized, when the noise shook the bars.

More crashes followed, filling the air outside the window of their cell with the sounds of metal and glass warping and shattering. It sounded like a traffic accident, but as the noise persisted and the wreck continued, Push wondered if cars weren't somehow being piled up on top of one another.

A horrible sinking feeling filled the pit of his stomach as it occurred to him that might be exactly what was going on. Push remembered that they had all recently encountered something with the power to do just that.

"I think maybe those microbots reactivated themselves sooner than you expected," Wrath told Professor Trixter in a calm voice.

The sound of several cars being knocked across a road into one another like marbles followed, making Scarlet Queen wince.

"I'm glad none of us were on the road today," she said.

Push and Scratch stepped forward, intent on getting a glimpse of what was happening through the window. Being closer, Professor Trixter beat them to it.

"They shouldn't have reassembled a body for themselves already," Trixter said, while Wiccan Witch led Wrath away so Scratch and Push could get a better look through the small window.

Push caught the sudden frown on Trixter's face. "What?" he asked before looking out the window at the scene unfolding.

"Unless," Trixter began, but Push cut him off.

"Get back!" he shouted, leaping away from the wall.

Scratch seized Professor Trixter by the arm, dragging him away as well. Wrath hadn't needed more warning than that. Scarlet Queen and Wiccan Witch had found themselves sandwiched between the bars on the other side of the cell and Wrath's tall frame. Push couldn't see their faces but imagined Scarlet looking less than thrilled.

An SUV struck the wall outside their cell, derailing Push's train of thought. The blow wasn't enough to shatter the wall, though it did crack the brick structure. More damaging was the momentum from the vehicle striking the building. Push felt the recoil slam into both him and Scratch, pitching them forward into the bars. The bars then let loose a horrible squeal. Unexpectedly, all six members of the team found themselves falling forward out of the cell into the corridor outside.

The bars, it turned out, were too tall to fall flat on the ground. Instead, the top part struck the wall while the bottom half slid along the concrete floor. Push and the others ended up dog piled on top of one another with their bodies lying halfway out of the cell.

"Remind me to personally thank the sheriff for getting the lowest bidder to renovate this place," Wrath muttered, getting off Scarlet Queen and Wiccan Witch and helping each one up.

"The SUV hitting the side of the building must have knocked the hinges loose," Push said over the noise, giving Scratch and Trixter a hand.

"Good observation," Trixter retorted. "So now that we're out, what's the game plan? Do we lock ourselves back up and pretend this didn't happen?"

Further noises came from outside. Push hadn't gotten a very good look at what was attacking cars out in the street, but a quick glance was enough for him to know they needed to move fast.

"Outside," he said. "That thing's attacking commuters in the road. Whatever the sheriff thinks, we've still got a job to do."

No one argued.

"I've got some good news," Trixter said, as they all moved down the short corridor one after the other. "In between all the phone calls we were making the last couple of days, I think I managed to come up with a virus that'll shut the nanobots—"

"Microbots," Wrath corrected.

"Not now," Scratch fired back.

"Whatever," Trixter said, sighing. "Shut the machines down. It hasn't been tested, of course, but now seems like a good time."

"Great," Wrath said. "Too bad the door is locked."

Wrath had gotten ahead of the others and was now standing in front with one hand on the knob, looking back at Push as though waiting for instructions.

"Do it," he said.

"Like you need permission," Scarlet Queen barked at him. "Blow the damn thing off its hinges so we can go."

"No one's going anywhere!"

The shout came from the other side of the door. Push recognized the voice as belonging to Deputy Fortenberry. Sure enough, a second later, his pudgy head appeared in the window on the other side.

"Sheriff sent me to check the prisoners," he said, like they were too simpleminded to figure that much out. "You bunch just get your asses back into that cell."

Wrath raised one hand, intent on burning his way through the door to get at Fortenberry's fat neck, but Push stopped him.

"Allow me," he said instead, motioning for the others to get as far back against the wall out of his way as they could.

Fortenberry's piggy eyes squinted, then widened in fear as Push summoned up a large chunk of his willpower and sent it flying at the door. Both it and Fortenberry were sent flying backward, the door ripping off its hinges in a manner similar to the cell they'd just vacated.

Push thought the crash that came was satisfying.

"Don't get up," said Wrath, as he and the others stepped over Fortenberry's bloated, half-conscious body one after the other.

"Yeah," said Scarlet Queen. "We'll see ourselves out."

"Have a nice day," Wiccan Witch threw in, earning her a look from Scarlet. "I couldn't think of anything more clever, and we're sort of pressed for time."

Something else, most likely another vehicle, struck the building, rattling it again.

"Outside," Scratch ordered. "And fast."

Nobody argued. Push expected someone else to stop them as they reached the doors, but the way was clear. The entire sheriff's department, save for Fortenberry, was gathered outside in the parking lot. In the distance near the main road was the mechanical beast Push had gotten a glimpse of through the window.

"It's...."

Scarlet Queen stopped short of any further description.

"Smaller," Wrath finished.

Smaller, Push observed, in comparison to the Trash Titans they'd fought before. The microbots were evidently going for a more compact approach this time around. The mechanized creature was stumbling around on six legs, each of which had wheels attached near the bottom. The body resembled something vaguely insectoid, if slightly misshapen.

Push thought he recognized the bodies of several vehicles smashed together, as if crumpled up like aluminum foil. The head was the most put-together part, like the robots had taken great care to make that above all else.

Mobility, however, was still something the beast was working on. Push saw that, despite being impressive, the thing didn't possess much in the way of maneuverability. The reason it had been having so much trouble, it seemed, was that cars kept getting in the way.

"Um, it doesn't look like it can get around very easily," Scratch noted, sounding a little underwhelmed.

"Maybe it was trying something different," Trixter suggested, thinking hard as he stroked his chin. "Thinking this form would better suit it."

"It did some things a little wrong," Scarlet Queen replied.

"Never mind any of that right now," Push barked, giving them each looks like they should know better. "Those people are getting hurt."

As though to emphasize the point, the metal monstrosity slammed the tip of one of its legs down onto the hood of an approaching car, stopping it short and deploying the air bags inside the front compartment.

"Right," said Wrath dryly. "I knew there was something we should be doing."

"Who let you bunch out?"

Push didn't bother turning around. The ire in Sheriff Black's voice was easy to identify by now. "No one," he said, not breaking his stride with the others, who walked side by side with him toward the mayhem. "The bars on the cell fell off. We thought we'd give your boys a hand."

Black's footsteps were echoing after them, barely audible above the chaos they were marching toward.

"Um, it doesn't look as though your boys are handling the situation very well," Scratch added, shooting Black a glare over his shoulder.

Wiccan Witch turned far enough to catch the sheriff's attention. "Shouldn't they be doing something right now?" she inquired, indicating the uniformed men who were still standing slack-jawed in the parking lot. "Like helping the people trapped in those cars, for example?"

That managed to snap the sheriff out of it.

"Lot!" he barked loudly over the din. "Get your ass in gear! Those people need help, goddammit!"

Push and his friends left the sheriff behind to yell orders at his troops. "That could have gone much worse," he said, once they were a few steps out of earshot.

Scarlet Queen snorted. "Even they aren't dumb enough to arrest us in the middle of all this," she replied.

"They're petty enough," Wrath countered warningly.

"Worry about it later," Push directed as they reached the big metal beast. "We've got other priorities. Wrath, turn up the heat."

Wrath stopped short of the road and rolled his sleeves up. Seeing what he was doing, the others began backing away to give him room to work. The gigantic metal cricket—for up close, Push thought it did resemble a cricket—took note of Wrath just as he flung a great ball of fire into the monster's left eye.

"That's good for you two," Scarlet Queen said, moving over to where Push had relocated with Scratch and Wiccan Witch, "but what are the rest of us supposed to do? We don't have our weapons."

Push looked at Professor Trixter. "I don't suppose you managed to grab anything before the cops dragged us all away."

Trixter started to open his mouth but then looked over the top of Push's head as a bright flash lit up the street. Push felt his own frustration rise, for it reminded him of how short he was.

"I don't think we need them," he replied, looking impressed. "Looks like your boy's handling the situation just fine."

Push caught the look on Scratch's face and flushed red. "He's not my boy," Push replied, a little angrier than he'd meant.

Another flash came, and Push whirled around to see what Wrath was up to. The pyrokinetic had gone for the joints where the thing's legs were connected. Remembering now how the metal cricket beast had stumbled about, as though having problems maneuvering, Push broke into a smile.

Wrath had summoned the same flame whip he'd used during the fight with Sloth and was striking away at the spot where the legs appeared weaker. The metal cricket was trying to fight back but moved far too slowly to catch something much smaller than it was. Wrath dodged out of the way as its front legs slammed down. A terrible sound of metal scraping against metal filled the air, and the two front legs promptly snapped apart.

Push spotted his chance and fired a telekinetic blast right into the thing's upper torso before it could fall flat on top of Wrath. Wrath jumped back but kept both eyes on the beast as it collapsed on its side. Only after it broke apart and the pieces didn't move did he turn to face Push.

"Thanks," Wrath told Push once he'd walked close enough. "But I could have handled it."

"You could have handled being street pizza?" Push countered good-naturedly.

"Why did it fall to pieces?" Scarlet Queen wondered, observing the pile of scrap as though it might come alive again, which was entirely possible.

"The nanobots—" Professor Trixter began.

"Microbots," Push interjected, only to look apologetically at Trixter afterward. "Sorry."

Trixter rolled his eyes. "The nanobots," he spat emphatically, "abandoned the body, it looks like. My guess is they gave up and went back to the drawing board."

That made Push frown. "Explain," he said, sharing a dark, worried look with Scratch. "Why would they give up?"

"Because they're learning," Trixter replied, like it was perfectly clear. "The microbots—"

"Ha!" Scarlet Queen shot at him. "You said 'microbots'!"

"A little decorum for right now," Wiccan Witch suggested coolly. "Now really isn't the time to debate semantics."

"Whatever," Trixter muttered, losing patience. "Remember when they first built those great big bodies for themselves? Those Trash Titans?"

This earned Trixter several odd looks.

"Um, not really the kind of thing anyone would forget," Scratch pointed out.

"True enough," admitted Trixter. "What I'm saying is, they went big on their first try, probably because they were programmed to do damage. That didn't work out, though, so the robots went smaller. Hence, we get our metalsect."

Everyone looked, as though waiting for an explanation.

"Meta-what?"

Push agreed with Scratch. "Metalsex?" he wondered aloud. "That sounds like a late-eighties thrasher-punk band."

"Metalsect," Professor Trixter clarified. "It's made of metal and shaped like an insect."

No one seemed to know what to make of that.

"So the microbots are learning to make better bodies for themselves," Wiccan Witch summarized, looking to get the conversation back on track. "They're getting smarter and stronger?"

"What's getting stronger?"

All six of them looked and saw Sheriff Black approaching. In spite of the noise still going on around them and the sound of approaching ambulances, the sheriff was still able to eavesdrop.

"The robots," Wrath informed him, pointing at the remains of the one he'd just taken apart with Push's help. "They're getting smarter."

"And stronger," Professor Trixter added. "That was just a test flight for them. More will be back, and they won't go down as easy."

Black's eyes widened. "This," he said, looking around at the wreckage of vehicles still littering the street. "This was easy? For you bunch, this was easy?"

"Um, 'fraid so," Scratch answered.

No one said a word at first. "So," Push said, hoping he wasn't about to make a mistake, for the sake of himself and his friends. "Are we still under arrest?"

CHAPTER
TWO

THEY WERE not under arrest. At least not for the moment.

Push let out a deep sigh of relief at the thought. He was currently sandwiched between Scarlet and Scratch as they worked their way down a sterile white hallway.

"I hate hospitals."

Push couldn't help but smirk at Scarlet Queen's flat tone of voice. A nurse happened to pass by them, going in the opposite direction. The man's eyes remained fixed straight ahead, as if he was afraid to look their way. It was the first sign of any personnel they'd come across since reaching that particular wing. Overall, the area felt deserted, like the place had been evacuated recently.

"Um, everyone hates hospitals," Scratch replied. "Even the doctors don't like coming here."

"How do you know that?" Push asked Scratch.

Push looked down and saw that their bodies had drifted closer together.

"Have you ever met a doctor or nurse that was excited about the idea of being in a hospital?" Scratch asked pointedly, snapping Push back to attention.

"I did, once," Scarlet Queen said, frowning suddenly. "And it was weird. I wanted to be transferred to a different facility after hearing him go on and on about how much he enjoyed his work."

"Um, when was this?" Scratch wondered.

Push winced as soon as he heard her reply. "Back when we were dating," Scarlet Queen answered easily. "The man was a gynecologist."

"Okay," Push agreed, forgetting why he'd been uncomfortable before. "That sounds really creepy."

"No kidding." Scarlet Queen went quiet for a moment, keeping her feet in step with both men as she looked from one to the other. "There's no reason to be nervous," she assured Push out of the blue. "I'm not jealous. You two make a cute couple."

The revelation startled Push. Scratch, on the other hand, smiled in an almost smug sort of way.

"You might want to remind him of that," Scratch told her while giving Push a teasing look. "I was telling him something along the same lines, but it didn't register."

Push's face glowed red as the three of them rounded a corner. "I just…," he tried, stammering. "I didn't want you to think…. I…."

Scratch and Scarlet Queen laughed loudly as Push trailed off. "Fair enough," Push said, snickering in spite of himself. "I guess we needed that. None of us want to be here."

Scarlet Queen's face fell abruptly. "Yeah," she admitted, rubbing an arm reflexively. "Especially if the description Wrath gave is still in effect. From the way he made it sound, this isn't going to be pretty."

Push's body twitched. "It won't be," he affirmed. "I wish there was another way."

It wasn't an ideal plan, but the best anyone could come up with given their resources. For the time being, Sheriff Black was back on their side. The Shove Point officers were currently patrolling for signs of more metalsects. Trixter seemed pretty confident that more were on the way.

At the moment, Trixter was preparing. The virus he'd developed to shut off the microbots was being loaded into the same spinning discs Push had watched him use when the robots had first attacked. The idea was for the virus to be transmitted into the microbots' system via an electric pulse. This also meant their brain trust would be tied up for the next couple of hours while the team was divided into two parts.

Wiccan Witch was taking Wrath with her to search for the pod. It seemed like a lesser concern at the moment, but Push wasn't about to let anyone, least of all himself, forget that several dangerous criminals were on the loose. Finding the pod would bring them one step closer to locating Sloth, Lust, and Envy, and finding them would bring the team closer to learning what the pod was for, and perhaps who the traitor in the Association was.

All of their Blackberry phones were linked, meaning they could be reached at a moment's notice if trouble reared its ugly, inconvenient head. Push expected it would soon enough. He would have liked to do something more constructive. The plan had been for both teams to search while they waited to hear from Black about microbot activity. Then Sheriff Black had dropped a serious bomb.

Duane was still in town at the hospital.

"The chopper was supposed to pick him up the other day," Black had said, looking a little put out over the fact, "after the incident at the pizza place and... so forth."

It felt gratifying that the sheriff was having trouble acknowledging his mistake in wanting to run them all out of town.

"I've been trying to speak to somebody about it," he'd gone on to say, "but keep getting the brush-off."

That had been the extent of their conversation and the clinching of Push's decision to keep hunting Sloth and the other remaining Deadly Seven. Wrath had been selected to search for the pod since he had the most experience with his former supervillain teammates. Wiccan Witch had volunteered to go with him, which Push had been grateful for. The idea of leaving Wrath alone to face any other Deadly Seven members made Push uneasy for more than one reason. Wiccan Witch's enthusiasm had earned her a snort from Scarlet Queen, something Push meant to ask her about.

"I'm having second thoughts," Scarlet Queen confessed, snapping Push out of his thoughts.

"This won't take long," Scratch said, though he looked at Push for confirmation. "Um, what makes you think he'll be able to talk?"

Push sighed heavily. "Nothing, really," he said sadly, thinking back to Duane's violent transformation. "I'm not sure that he can talk still. Whatever was happening to him before, it was still going on when Wrath and I took him down. But I want to at least try before the Association airlifts him away."

"At least you'll have the chance," Scratch said, slowing his pace along with the others as they reached their destination. "Thanks to the bombings, the Association has been too busy to think about Duane."

"That," Scarlet Queen chimed in warningly, "or our mole is somehow keeping certain things from getting to the people that need them. Like information."

It was a terrifying thought, and one that deserved more consideration. Push resolved to dwell on that further once the current multiple-choice crisis had tapered off. Hesitating outside the door to the special unit that had been set aside specifically for Duane, who until recently had been known as the Pranksta Gayngsta, Push thought back on the events of the last week or so.

Duane had been why Push, Scratch, and Wrath had come to the two-story town of Shove Point in the first place. Someone had paid the guy to masquerade as a bank-robbing practical joker, a la some villain from a Silver Age comic book. Wrath had helped Push and Scratch put him away, but the Pranksta Gayngsta was able to escape in a matter of hours.

As a result, the Association had seen fit to assign all three men the task of chasing the Pranksta Gayngsta down to the boondocks of the Deep South. That was the official version, though Push had received conflicting reports since then, particularly one about them being relocated to Shove Point in disgrace because they'd fucked up.

Duane had shown up on their doorstep several days ago. To say that the man had looked worse for wear would be an understatement. Sloth had done something to the poor guy, something awful, and the result was waiting for them behind those doors.

Push swallowed the lump that had formed in his throat and reached forward, pressing the call button on the wall next to the entrance.

A moment later, one of the nurses appeared in the small glass window. "No one is allowed inside," she said loudly through the face mask. "This area is under quarantine."

Push held up his Association ID. "We're with the Real-Life Superhero Association," he announced, knowing full well that part was obvious, thanks to their uniforms. "We were all around the subject during the early stages of his transformation. If his condition were contagious, it would have affected us way before now."

Scarlet Queen grimaced at the thought.

"We just want to come inside and question him for a minute before the transport chopper arrives," Push went on.

He'd avoided calling Duane "the subject" a second time. That was something.

The nurse, meanwhile, didn't look convinced, yet her eyes softened slightly when Scratch spoke up.

"We're hoping he remembers something else about what changed him," Scratch added. "If we knew that, it might help change him back."

"Please," Scarlet Queen added.

Slowly, the nurse backed away. "Wait there a moment," she said before walking away out of Push's sight.

Scarlet Queen folded both arms in front of her. "What are the odds of us getting in?" she asked, keeping one eye on the small window.

"Based on what we've been through in this town so far," Scratch replied sourly, "um, not very high. More than likely, she just went to find someone to throw us out."

The thought had already crossed Push's mind, but he wasn't about to leave without confirming with his own eyes that Duane's condition had stabilized.

"At least he wasn't contagious," Push said. "That was really stupid of me, letting everybody go off when we weren't even sure if Duane's condition would spread to other people."

"There was a lot going on," Scratch replied at once, coming to Push's defense. "Shit, there's still a whole hell of a lot going on. That's why we agreed to split into two teams. Professor Trixter is wrapping stuff up with the virus, and Wrath and Wiccan Witch have got a head start looking for Sloth and that pod while we square stuff away here."

Scratch's voice turned unexpectedly sour when he mentioned Wrath's name.

"That," Scarlet Queen added, interrupting Push's train of thought, "and none of us wanted to watch Wrath and Wiccan Witch make goo-goo eyes at one another."

"What?" Push turned toward Scarlet Queen with a stunned look. "Why would they make—"

The whole building shook abruptly, cutting Push off. Dust rained down onto their uniforms from the ceiling as what sounded like an explosion rocked the air. Push's eyes widened as, through the small glass window, he saw a different nurse stagger.

"The hell?" Scarlet Queen swore, righting herself.

"It came from in there," Scratch said, nodding at the door as he whipped out the new, specially crafted cue stick Professor Trixter had made, from his long coat.

"I know," Push replied. "Stand back."

Neither group member needed to be told twice. Push thrust his palm out as they jumped back, and let loose with a powerful telekinetic force bubble. The invisible blast hit the double doors, knocking them right off their hinges and setting off an alarm.

Scarlet Queen glanced around at the noise. "An explosion does nothing," she commented, "but one door gets knocked off its hinges and the whole place goes on high alert."

"Welcome to Shove Point," Scratch replied. "It's gets weirder."

The three didn't get far inside before coming to a stop. The source of the explosion was straight ahead. The area was more or less a great rectangular chamber. Smaller rooms with glass walls had been built around the edges, save for the far wall on the other end. Part of said wall had been obliterated by what Push assumed was heavy explosives. Rubble and shrapnel surrounded a gaping hole, and in front of it stood two familiar faces.

"Who are these guys?" Scarlet Queen asked.

Scratch raised his cue stick. "Sloth," he introduced, pointing at each one, "and Lust, the remains of the Deadly Seven. They're the bad guys."

Sloth heard this and snorted, tossing the pale dreadlocks away from his albino face. "Ignore them," he instructed Lust, who stood just behind Sloth's oversized frame on his right. "We're here for the weapon."

"The girl's pretty," Lust said, running his tongue over the surface of the dagger he held in front of him. "I want her."

Scarlet Queen raised her left arm in answer. "Bad guys," she said as the laser crossbow Professor Trixter had given her unfolded with the press of a switch. "Got it."

The crossbow fired, striking Lust squarely in the torso. Scarlet Queen fired several more times, covering Lust's short, lanky body with laser burns.

Sloth shifted slightly and watched as Scarlet Queen ceased fire, bringing the crossbow up to her lips to blow on it.

"You didn't tell me they'd been given new toys," Lust grunted, getting back onto his feet slowly. "That actually hurt."

Both daggers were still clutched in Lust's hands. "I liked it," he grinned.

Push sent out a telekinetic blast that sent Lust flying backward through the hole he and Sloth had blown in the wall.

Scarlet Queen shot Push a glare. "No fair," she said irritably. "I wanted to do that."

Sloth, meanwhile, was backing up slowly toward the exit. "Don't move," Push warned, keeping his hands up as he and the others stepped forward.

"Or what?" Sloth called back tauntingly. "You'll shoot me? That isn't any of your style."

"We can still hurt you," Scratch said confidently.

This made Sloth laugh. "The last time, you two could barely fight me," he reminded, still backing away. "You've got some new toys, I'll give you that, but you're still nowhere near my league. Get back to me when you've got the firebug with you. He knows how to throw down. The rest of you are just kids playing cops and robbers in bad Halloween costumes."

That statement got Scarlet Queen's attention, and she opened fire. Sloth stared down at the smoldering hole that formed in his shirt near the solar plexus.

"That almost tickled," he said in a calm voice.

"This guy's got thicker skin," Scratch told her, pulling out two of his trick balls. "It takes more punch to get through to him."

Sloth was grinning. Lust, meanwhile, had crawled back into the room with blood running down his face and a mad gleam in his eye. "Speaking of thick skin," said Sloth, holding up what looked like a small detonator switch. "Let's see just how much pain you 'heroes' can withstand."

Push's eyes widened in shock as Sloth's thumb mashed down on the red button. All three of them recoiled, bracing for impact. The world should have exploded all around them. That was what Push had been expecting, at least. Instead, someone started screaming.

And Push felt his blood grow cold. The voice that was crying out sounded very familiar.

"You never build a weapon without an off switch," Sloth said as Push and the others straightened back up. "Or without a leash to keep it in line."

"I would have volunteered," Lust said, his eyes practically shining with eagerness as the cries continued, "but boss man has this thing about taking the short road."

Scarlet Queen stared grimly at the room not far from where they stood. A figure inside was thrashing about in agony. The cries were coming from inside. Without Push telling her, she'd worked out that it was Duane. Push was watching as well, along with Scratch. Somehow, Sloth was able to hurt him from a distance.

"Stop it," Scratch said, looking at Sloth furiously. "Just cut it out already. The man's been hurt enough."

Lust snorted. "Not nearly enough yet," he declared, holding a knife up. "But we'll soon fix that."

"You must have figured it out by now," Sloth went on, ignoring Lust. "The microbots I injected his body with were tearing him down from the inside out, making him into a living weapon. The procedure was dangerous, painful, and illegal of course. With a press of this switch, I can order them to take him apart bit by bit."

"It's like having all your favorite classic hits loaded into an iPod," Lust said, giggling. "Any chance I can get an audio file of this later?"

Sloth answered by backhanding Lust. Lust flew back into the broken wall, knocking a piece of it away before landing on his ass halfway outside.

"Fine," Lust grumbled. "Don't tell me I can't take a hint."

"What do you want?" Push demanded as Duane's screams grew louder.

"What I came here for," Sloth said. "I take the package with me. None of you so much as take one step after us. Or we can stand here and listen as the Pranksta Gayngsta's body dissolves over the next couple of hours."

Push eyed the switch in Sloth's hand. Scarlet Queen glanced his way, signaling him with her eyes that she'd thought of the same thing.

"Don't bother," Sloth replied, catching on. "I've got backups, and this isn't some corny TV series. Smashing the switch won't turn the microbots off. They don't need a constant signal. Just a command code broadcast once through the airwaves."

"Fine," Push consented, hating himself the whole time.

Taking two steps back for good measure, Push motioned for Scarlet Queen and Scratch to do the same. Neither looked pleased by this turn of events, but both followed his lead. Sloth watched the whole time, wearing a satisfied smile.

"Lust," he said.

Lust had been getting to his feet and stumbled back over to where Sloth was. "You didn't have to hit me so hard," he muttered.

"Get the weapon," Sloth ordered, his voice leaving no room for debates. "We're leaving."

Lust looked startled by this. "All by myself?" he demanded unhappily. "That sick freak's got to be twice my weight by now. At least!"

Sloth glared down at Lust but then considered the knife fighter's words. "You have a point," he said, casually tossing the switch over to Lust.

Lust caught the switch in midair, only to find himself on the receiving end of another one of Sloth's backhands.

"I'll get him instead," Sloth said calmly as Lust rolled to a stop near the hole.

Push kept his eyes on Sloth as the hulking man glided easily over to the room where Duane was thrashing around in pain on top of the hospital bed. Scratch was doing his part by keeping Lust in his sights. Scarlet Queen was shooting both looks of pure loathing.

"What do we do?" she asked quietly as Duane let out a particularly gruesome howl.

Push answered by thrusting his palm out. Lust's eyes bulged in shock a second before the invisible force bubble slammed into him. The crunch that filled the room as the lanky man crashed against the wall behind him felt satisfying. No one needed further instructions. Scratch and Scarlet Queen charged forward together while Push flanked off to the side toward Sloth.

Sloth had turned around, but Push was one step ahead of him, sliding past along the freshly waxed floor to block the entrance to Duane's room. Scratch, meanwhile, snatched the switch up off the floor as Scarlet Queen shoved her Taser club into Lust's chest. Duane's screams fell silent as Lust's took their place.

"Fucking Christ," Sloth grumbled while Push stood with his telescopic bo in both hands, guarding Duane's room. "Don't you people ever give up?"

Push opened his mouth, intending to answer with a witty remark, but was cut off as Sloth pulled a second switch out of his pocket, his thumb already pushing down on it. Fresh cries, these weaker than before, came from behind Push.

"We can do this all day," Sloth told him calmly. "How long do you think you can bear to listen to that man dying?"

Scarlet Queen was forced back suddenly as Lust first kicked out with his foot, then swiped one of his knives dangerously close to her throat.

"Stupid bitch," he jeered, rolling backward to his feet. "Pain is my friend. Let me introduce you to some of it."

"No thanks," Scarlet Queen replied, drawing her sword.

Scratch opened fire with the laser built into the tip of his cue stick, but Lust was already dodging out of the way. Push remembered that Lust's ability was hyperkinetic reflexes, meaning he was able to dodge just about anything people threw at him, including bullets.

Push watched, carefully dividing his time between Sloth and the fight just a few short feet away, as Scratch let go of the cue stick with one hand to press the switch he held. Duane's screaming stopped yet again. Sloth was also keeping track of things and rolled his eyes.

"This is so juvenile," he scoffed. "Don't you three have something better to do than waste my time?"

"Nope," Push countered confidently.

Sloth hit the switch in his hand again. Duane's screaming started up once more in response, making Push wince.

"All that stress from turning the pain on and off can't be good for him," said Sloth, back to being calm. "Even a weapon has limitations."

"He's not a weapon, Sloth," Push asserted.

"He's a freak of bad technology," Sloth retorted. "A science project cooked up by a bunch of lonely geeks for a bunch of glory hounds. You and I are both seen as weirdos, but the poor bastard in the room you're guarding has us both beaten in the monster department."

"What?" Push wondered, while Scratch and Scarlet Queen ganged up on a ricocheting Lust, who kept evading their attacks by flipping back and forth.

Push had forgotten how well they worked together.

"What?" he demanded, turning his attention back to Sloth again. "That's your Freudian excuse for ruining a man's life? Your parents didn't love you and they thought you were a monster?"

Sloth laughed, a loud belly roll.

"Don't be so stupid," he chided. "This is all business for me."

The two of them had been standing close together for several minutes. There was maybe four feet between their bodies. During that whole time, Sloth hadn't moved an inch. Suddenly, the albino's body lunged forward, and Push remembered seconds too late Wrath's warning about Sloth being faster than he looked. The fist that hammered into his stomach knocked the wind straight out of him. Sloth spun around, the movement as graceful as any stage dancer, bringing his leg up into a kick that connected with Push's shoulder.

The blow sent Push tumbling sideways into a stack of what might have been hospital supplies. He was too dazed to be sure. The noise that followed caught the attention of the others just in time to watch Push hitting his head on the floor. Everything after that was a blur.

Push tried to get up, but his limbs weren't being very cooperative. The blow to his head had scrambled his brain. Gritting his teeth, he forced his body to move as Scratch cried out in what sounded like pain.

That got the adrenaline going.

"What did I say about killing?" Sloth's voice suddenly boomed in anger. "They're not to be damaged too much."

"Party pooper," Lust shot back.

Push raised up in time to watch Sloth racing out through the blown wall with what might have been Duane slung over one shoulder and Lust being dragged along behind by the scruff of his neck. Not far away was Scarlet Queen leaning over a bleeding Scratch.

Push's mind snapped into gear.

"Scratch!"

"He's all right," Scarlet Queen assured him. "He took the knife in the shoulder, but the bleeding is pretty bad."

"We've got a hurt man," Push shouted over his shoulder.

The area was empty of people save for themselves. "The hell is everyone?" Push wondered, looking back at Scratch again, who was wearing an apologetic expression.

"He's fast," Scratch grunted as Push touched his shoulder gingerly. "I thought I could get the drop on him."

Push kissed the side of his head. "You dumb fuck," he said, halfway between panic and relief that Scratch wasn't hurt worse. "Always doing something risky."

"Like standing up to a guy three times your size?" Scratch replied pointedly.

"Doctor," Scarlet Queen called out abruptly.

Push turned around and saw a man in a white coat entering behind several hospital personnel. "We've got a man down," she continued. "Stab wound to the shoulder."

The doctor came forward without a word. Push recognized the man as Hamilton, the same doctor that had been in the ER when Duane's transformation kicked in.

"I'm going after Sloth," Scarlet Queen told Push after the doctor had waved them back so he could look Scratch over.

"Just follow," Push ordered her. "You and Scratch together couldn't take Lust down, and Sloth is supposed to be worse. Just see if you can locate their hideout. Then report back."

Scarlet Queen started to argue but then looked down again as Scratch let out a hiss. "We need to get him to the ICU," Hamilton was saying. "Someone bring a stretcher."

It dawned on Push that he should be going with Scarlet Queen, but one look from her said everything.

"Don't even think about it," she said. "Stay with him. I promise to try and stay out of trouble for once so you don't have more to feel bad about."

"Do I get a say in this?" Scratch asked as Hamilton began helping him onto the stretcher.

"No," both Push and Scarlet Queen said at the same time.

"You stay here and make sure he doesn't do anything I would," Scarlet Queen told Push, "like try to follow me. I'll report in regularly."

"You'll have to sit in one of the waiting rooms," Hamilton interjected as the team started to wheel Scratch off on the stretcher. "Unless either of you is family."

"I'm his boyfriend," Push answered, and it struck him just how easy the words flowed out of his mouth.

Hamilton actually looked sympathetic. "Sorry," he said. "Family only."

Push couldn't help scowling as he watched the man he loved being wheeled out of sight. "Stay anyway," Scarlet Queen advised. "Just to be on the safe side. You said Wrath had sensed that Envy weirdo in here a few days back. If he's still hiding in the hospital, none of us should be here alone."

"Right," Push agreed, though he wasn't happy with Scarlet Queen going off on her own. "Good thinking."

Scarlet Queen nodded and gave a little salute before taking off through the exit Sloth and Lust had formed. Watching her go, Push whipped out his Blackberry and hit the button for Wrath.

"Scratch, Scarlet Queen, and I just got our asses handed to us by Sloth and Lust," he said once Wrath answered. "They got away with Duane, so I'm hoping you have some good news for us right about now."

"We do," Wrath replied. "Hold on, though. I think I can link the call with Wiccan Witch's phone so you don't have to explain things twice."

Push took off for the door after Scratch while Wrath fiddled with his phone. Wiccan Witch's voice could be heard in the background, and it sounded like she was giving Wrath instructions.

"Sorry that took so long," Wiccan Witch said after a particularly loud beep. "Are you guys okay?"

"Scratch took a knife to the shoulder," Push explained, "but I think he's going to be fine. Scarlet Queen left to try and track down Sloth and Lust. I want to go with her, but we can't afford to leave Scratch alone right now."

"You're in the hospital?" Wrath said, making it a question. "The same one where I sensed Envy before?"

"Right," Push replied as he followed a sign pointing toward the ICU. "If he's still around, Scratch might be in danger."

"Stay there," Wiccan Witch advised. "We'll come to you just as soon as we can. Professor Trixter just called, and he's on his way to pick us up in the hovercraft."

Push frowned.

"What for?" he wondered, coming up on the Intensive Care Unit now.

"We found that pod Sloth was looking for," Wrath answered, and it sounded like he was smiling now. "Only it's too big for both of us to carry. Trixter is going to give us a ride once he's done uploading the virus."

"See you soon," Push said, claiming a spot by the wall next to the ICU doors. "And make it fast. I don't want Scratch to be here any longer than he has to be. This place gives me the creeps."

"All hospitals are like that," Wiccan Witch said. "See you soon."

"WHAT KEPT you guys?"

Push was standing underneath the canopy outside the emergency entrance of the hospital. Scratch had taken a seat on one of the benches. One hand clutched clumsily at the bandaged knife wound. Push had spent the last half hour hovering over him nervously like a mother hen, knowing his boyfriend was okay, but anxious all the same.

Scratch had been treated and released in very short order. The knife wound wasn't pretty, but wasn't life threatening, either. Hamilton had prescribed some mild painkillers for Scratch to take over the next week and an antibiotic to prevent infection, along with orders to take it easy. Following that, there was nothing for the two to do but wait for the others.

Luckily, Professor Trixter's hovercraft was an eyesore. Several people inside the waiting room had spotted it coming and were lining up alongside the windows to watch.

"That pod was fucking heavy," Trixter replied irritably. "We wound up having to lower the backseats so it could fit. It's waiting for us back at the house."

"Um, you left it in the garage?" Scratch winced slightly as he reached reflexively with his left arm. "Shit, that still hurts."

Wiccan Witch eyed the wounded left shoulder as Wrath got the door for Scratch. "How bad is it?" she asked, looking back and forth between Scratch and Push.

"Thanks," Scratch said to Wrath as he climbed in. "It hurts, but I've managed worse before," he told Wiccan Witch as Push settled into the seat next to him. "The worst part is knowing I let that knife-wielding psycho get away."

"Lust was one of the Deadly Seven's top killers," Push said grimly. "I should never have let you and Scarlet Queen go toe-to-toe with him."

"Agreed," Wrath said flatly.

Wiccan Witch gave Wrath a sharp smack on the hand as she lowered herself into the seat beside him.

"Where is Scarlet Queen?" she asked, frowning.

"Following Sloth and Lust," Scratch answered before Push could. "Hopefully, she's found their hideout by now."

Push's Blackberry went off, as if in reply to Scratch's statement. Sure enough, it was from Scarlet Queen.

"Any news?" he asked, upon answering it.

"All bad," Scarlet Queen replied. "I lost them. They had a getaway vehicle stashed not far from the hospital. I tried to keep track but lost them on the highway. They're probably long gone."

Push started to reassure her, but something dawned on him. "How were you able to follow them on the highway?" he wondered, getting a bad feeling. "Professor Trixter had the hovercraft."

Scarlet Queen cleared her throat uncomfortably. "I talked this guy into letting me borrow his motorcycle," she said, clearly not giving Push all the details.

"Scarlet...."

"He gave it to me voluntarily," she insisted. "Eventually. In fact, I'm about to return it to him right now."

"You know where he is right now?"

Once again, Scarlet Queen coughed nervously into the phone. "Actually, he came along for the ride. I couldn't get him to hand over the keys, so we reached a compromise."

Push groaned.

"Can you guys come pick me up?" she asked, and Push could hear the other man talking in the background. "This guy says he's got a wedding or something to go to."

Push got the address and fired it off to Professor Trixter, who punched the coordinates into the GPS computer.

"What happened?" Wrath asked curiously.

"Nothing," Push replied. "We've got to make a quick detour to pick up Scarlet Queen before we go get Scratch's prescription filled. That's all."

Wiccan Witch didn't look convinced. "What did she do this time?"

"Nothing," Push said a little too quickly. "But let's hurry anyway."

Scratch was laughing the whole time. Either he'd overhead the phone call or was just that intimately familiar with Scarlet Queen's antics. Push wasn't sure, but hearing his boyfriend laugh brought a smile to his face.

The address Scarlet Queen had given led them to the other side of Shove Point. Scarlet Queen was waiting at a corner next to a stop sign and waved as the hovercraft rolled to a stop. A young-looking man standing next to a bright-red motorcycle waved enthusiastically as they drove off.

"Don't ask," she said when Wiccan Witch opened her mouth.

"I was just going to ask if you gave him your number," Wiccan Witch replied defensively.

Push and Scratch laughed along with Professor Trixter.

"No," Scarlet Queen replied haughtily. "I gave him yours instead."

To Push's surprise, Wiccan Witch patted Wrath affectionately on the leg. "I'll pass," she said. "You'll have to go out with him instead. I've already made other plans."

Even more surprisingly, Wrath glanced back out the window at the young man still watching in the distance.

"Too bad," he told Wiccan Witch in a playful tone. "He was cute."

Push rolled his eyes and faced forward in his seat until they arrived at the local Walmart. Scratch's prescription took another hour to get filled. During that time, Push checked in with Sheriff Black to see if there had been any more metalsect attacks. Thus far, it had been quiet on that front, but Push was far from relieved. The longer the microbots waited to reassemble bodies for themselves, the more dangerous they potentially were.

Meanwhile, Push was getting quite a few looks from the other customers. Scratch had taken him up on the offer to wait inside the hovercraft while Push shopped for him. Now Push was regretting the decision. Scratch might have been injured, but some of the looks Push kept getting were outright odd. Granted, he was in uniform at the moment. Costumed heroes tended to draw a crowd, and this was nothing unusual by itself. Push wouldn't have found it too strange if the locals were lining up to give him dirty glares.

What they were doing was laughing, as though the sight of a superhero picking up antibiotics at a Walmart pharmacy was the most hilarious thing ever. After a while, Push opted to ignore them. For whatever reason, the locals didn't think he was entitled to do normal things.

Wrath would be laughing his head off if he knew.

Sure enough, the newest Association member was grinning from ear to ear when Push climbed back into the hovercraft a while later. The others had similar expressions.

"Have fun?" Wrath asked pointedly.

Push refused to comment. Scratch looked like he wanted to bust a gut but maintained a stiff expression as their hands linked together.

"Let's head home so we can get you doped up," he said, facing Scratch. "Then we'll have a look at that pod."

"Right." Scratch grimaced as he climbed out of the hovercraft. "Where is it, anyway?"

"In the living room," Wiccan Witch said as Wrath unlocked the door. "We had to turn it sideways and heft it in through the back."

"The living room was the only space big enough to put it," Wrath added as the group filed in one after the other.

Sure enough, the pod was resting on top of a blanket on the living room floor behind the corner couch. Push caught a glimpse of it but set the problem aside in his head to focus on Scratch. Professor Trixter grabbed Scratch a seat while Wiccan Witch opened the bag with the painkillers and extra bandages that Push had picked up while waiting. Scratch obliged by not arguing with either of them and consenting to let Push help him out of his coat. Wiccan Witch then handed Scratch the glass of water and two pills, one antibiotic and one painkiller, before lifting Scratch's shirt up to begin changing his bandages.

Wrath, meanwhile, was busying himself in the other half of the kitchen. "It isn't going to be much," he told them idly while breaking out the cookware. "But we might as well eat while we have the chance."

Nobody argued. Push turned his focus back to Scratch while Wrath worked. Scratch was keeping still while Wiccan Witch peeled away the bloody bandage. Unable to help, Scarlet Queen and Professor Trixter vacated the room, choosing to loom around the pod.

Push would have joined them had Scratch not been hurt.

"I'm fine."

Scratch's voice startled him. "I'm fine, Push," his boyfriend insisted, grinning up at him. "You had that look on your face like you were worried."

Push's response was to blush.

"He really will be fine," Wiccan Witch assured, applying new bandages now. "The wound looks like it's already healing. I doubt he'll have to be benched."

"Like I'd let this stop me," Scratch retorted playfully. "We've got robots and aliens to fight. I'm not about to let a little cut stop me from doing what we've dreamed of doing since we were kids."

That made Push grin.

"Let's do it, then," he said, helping Scratch to his feet with one hand once Wiccan Witch had finished. "We're all due for some answers."

"Soup's on," Wrath declared. "While that heats, why don't we have a look at that pod and see what all the fuss is about."

"I'm game," said Wiccan Witch happily.

"Same here," agreed Scratch. "Let's go."

Push took Scratch by the hand and followed the others into the living room. His mood was brought down, however briefly, by the sight of Wiccan Witch and Wrath doing the same. The sight of the pod, though, changed that in short order.

"Is it safe to open that?" he wondered aloud.

"Probably not," Professor Trixter replied, looking excited. "I can't wait to split this baby in two so we can see what's inside."

Scarlet Queen was sharing in Trixter's enthusiasm. "How are you going to do it?" she asked, looking the pod over like a kid would a Christmas present. "Hack its mainframe?"

"Nope," Trixter said, holding what looked like a laser cutter in one hand. "We're doing this the old-fashioned way."

A thought occurred to Push as the rattling from Trixter's laser cutter filled the room. "Where'd you two find this thing at, anyway?" he asked Wiccan Witch and Wrath.

"I probably should have asked that earlier," he added, mumbling under his breath while Trixter continued working.

"You were worried about Scratch," Wiccan Witch replied pointedly. "Nothing to be ashamed of there."

"Right," Wrath agreed, though in a slightly drier tone. "To answer your question, we found it in the woods not far from this old farmhouse. Wiccan Witch was actually the one to lead us there, though."

"I conjured up a couple of old ghosts that were lurking in the woods," she explained, speaking as though that were the perfectly logical thing to do. "They said that something had landed near the farm but were a little sketchy on the details. Ghosts have a terrible sense of timing, you know."

"Of course," Push said, keeping his own thoughts on the subject quiet. "Go on."

"Not much else to tell," Wiccan Witch said, giving Wrath's forearm a squeeze, which didn't go unnoticed by Push. "The pod had fallen into a catfish pond. From the looks of it when we got there, it had just reactivated and washed halfway ashore."

"This thing has weird luck when it comes to water," Wrath noted, giving the pod a strange look before turning back to Push.

"So we phoned Trixter and had him come out with the hovercraft," Wiccan Witch finished. "But ask Wrath what he said about the farmhouse."

Push blinked and turned expectantly toward Wrath. "It's nothing," Wrath said, though he sounded less than certain. "Probably," he then threw in. "It looked like someone had been living on the farm recently. The place was derelict, but I definitely got the sense that people had been there, and regularly."

Push waited, but Wrath said nothing else. "Like who?" he pressed.

"Maybe Sloth," Wrath admitted. "I considered investigating, but it seemed like the pod took priority. If the farm is Sloth's hideout, we can always go back to it later."

Push nodded. "Good call," he praised, smiling. "We'll head out there and give the place a look-see once we're done here, and maybe have some of your soup."

Wrath looked stunned by Push's compliments. Wiccan Witch gave Wrath a smile like she was fighting off laughter while Push fished out his phone. "I've got to make a call," he said, leaving the room to escape the noise. "Be right back."

CHAPTER
THREE

"OKAY," PUSH said into the phone. "See you in a few minutes."

As the screen died, Push looked over at Professor Trixter, who was quietly swearing to himself as he wrestled with a section of the pod.

"Careful," Wrath warned. "You don't want to hurt… whatever might be inside."

"He's on his way," Push said, looking from Wrath to Trixter. "Are you sure you don't want our help?"

"I'm good," Trixter hissed out through clenched teeth. "It's… just a little stuck. That's all. Any minute now."

"I think this is a bad idea."

Push turned back to where Wrath and Wiccan Witch were watching on the couch. "I'm aware of how welcome my opinion is," Wrath continued before Push could say anything, "but I think bringing Black into this is a mistake."

"Because you don't like him?" Push asked, though not unkindly.

"No," Wrath replied, as though he'd been expecting that. "Or rather, I don't like him at all, but that isn't the reason. I think Black will sell us out if it means protecting Shove Point. He already sees us as the source of all the recent trouble."

Push said nothing for a moment, thinking over Wrath's words. Much as he hated to acknowledge it, Wrath had a point. Suddenly, Push wasn't sure inviting the sheriff over had been such a good idea. At the very least, he'd thought to ask Black to come alone.

"Still," Scarlet Queen said over more of Trixter's cursing. "We need to work alongside the local cops if we want to wrap this whole mess up. If we show—"

Scarlet Queen paused to glance over at the pod. "—whatever is in there to him," she continued, "it just might convince him that we're not a threat."

"Or get him off our backs," Scratch said in a tired voice.

It sounded to Push as though the painkillers were kicking in. "Agreed," Push said, looking at Scratch longer than he knew he should.

Though they were a couple now, and everyone knew it, this wasn't the time for him to be making goo-goo eyes at his injured boyfriend. Knowing that wasn't stopping Push from wanting to scoop Scratch up in his arms and snuggle with him under a blanket.

Push realized to his great embarrassment that he was still staring. Moreover, everyone else was watching him stare, including Professor Trixter.

"If you two need to be alone for a bit, go right ahead," Trixter stated in a weary voice. "This thing isn't going anywhere."

Push felt his face burn. Scratch, however, was watching him now, wearing a rather satisfied, almost catlike look.

"Promise you'll be gentle with me," Scratch said tauntingly. "I'm an injured man, after all."

Push felt his face burn brighter, if that were possible, but he rose to the challenge anyway. "Not a chance," he retorted, storming over to where Scratch sat and grabbing him by the hair. "Fast and hard, just the way I like it."

"Who's going first?" Wrath wondered.

Wiccan Witch gave Wrath a playful smack in answer, while Scarlet Queen tossed a sofa cushion his way. Wrath caught the cushion and placed it next to him without a word. Push ignored them and bent down to kiss Scratch. He could feel everyone's eyes on them as their mouths connected, but Push didn't care. The moment he could taste Scratch's breath on his lips, the world shrank away, leaving the two of them alone together.

Except for the doorbell, which rang three times at that precise moment, loud and impatiently.

"Fuck," Scratch swore around Push's mouth.

"Should have known," Push muttered, pulling away. "It's probably Sheriff Black. I'll go let him in."

Push got the door open just as Sheriff Black was getting ready to pound on it. "Come inside," Push said, stepping back so the sheriff could enter. "We've got some things to tell you."

The sheriff stopped short inside the living room. Push had forgotten that the sheriff was tall enough to see the big pod on the floor past the couch. Being a few inches over five feet, it was a little more difficult for Push without knowing what was there.

"I'd say you've got something to show me," Black said, taking a few tentative steps farther into the living room. "What in Sam Hill is that thing?"

"We're not exactly sure," Push said, closing the front door and following after the sheriff. "Wrath and Wiccan Witch found it in the woods earlier today. We knew it was somewhere here in Shove Point because…."

Push paused, thinking everything over.

"Actually," he decided, motioning for the sheriff to have a seat, "maybe I should start over from the beginning."

While Trixter continued working, Push launched into the story of everything that had happened so far. From the Clickers, those bipedal insectoid creatures they'd found scrounging through the plane wreckage in town, to the crashed ship on the lake shore in the woods.

"There's one other thing too," Push went on as Sheriff Black looked around the room at the others, as though expecting them to cry out "April Fool" or something. "We think one of the members of the Deadly Seven is hiding out at the hospital."

Black immediately turned to Wrath. "Sorry," Wrath told him coldly over the noise of Trixter's tools. "It isn't me."

"Wrath sensed the presence of Envy," Push went on, giving Wrath a cautionary look. "Envy was a master of disguise, and we don't know who he was pretending to be. It happened while we were in the ER with Duane, the former Pranksta Gayngsta."

"I heard," Black said, sighing. "You couldn't have waited for me to brief you all?"

"You never showed up," Scratch said, having to talk louder for the noise Trixter was making. It sounded like the strain was making him even more tired than the painkillers.

"This ain't *CSI: Miami*," Black fired back at him. "My boys have been too busy trying to fix the mess downtown from that plane crash and looking out for giant monsters. We're pushed to our breaking point as it is."

"We get that," Push said, jumping in before an argument could break out. From the looks of things, Scarlet Queen and Wrath were about to do that very thing.

"We're going to go out on patrol soon," Scratch interjected, taking the floor. "Trixter has the virus we need to shut down the nanobots—"

"Microbots," Trixter muttered under his breath.

"Whatever," said Scratch, rolling his eyes. "So that'll be wrapped up soon enough. We thought you should be brought up to speed on the situation. Working together will mean things get fixed a hell of a lot faster."

Black looked around the room again. Going by his expression, it didn't look as though he was pleased with the idea of an alliance. To everyone's surprise, he gave the room a small nod of consent before standing to leave.

"Let me know if you get that thingamajig cracked open," Black said on his way out the door. "I know some people who might be able to help, if you're interested."

Trixter didn't raise his head until he heard Black's vehicle start up outside. "All clear?" he asked, looking around the room.

Wrath stood up and marched over to a nearby window to peer out the blinds. "All clear," he announced. "What have you got?"

The grin on Trixter's face would have burned fiberglass. "This baby's sealed up pretty tight," he said, giving it a light smack. "Whoever built it didn't want anybody cracking it open."

"Did you hurt it?" Wrath asked, suddenly concerned. "I kept sensing something inside of it, like it was alive somehow."

Everyone's eyes widened at this.

"Why didn't you say so?" Wiccan Witch asked as Wrath sat back down next to her.

"It feels… different," he said, looking from her over to Push. "Like the life signs are almost nonexistent. I wasn't sure at first, but the longer I sat here, the more it felt like something alive is in there. I didn't say anything because I didn't think the sheriff should know."

Push scowled at this. "It's called trusting someone, Wrath," he said derisively. "If we want the sheriff on our side, we can't keep secrets from him."

Wrath said nothing but did not back down from Push's glare.

"Ahem," Trixter said, looking back and forth between them. "I'm about to do something very brilliant in a minute, so it'd be nice if you two could keep a lid on it until I'm done."

Nobody said anything.

"Good," Trixter declared. "I was making all that noise earlier to cover up what I was really doing."

Push gave Trixter a surprised look.

"He's not the only one who thinks the sheriff might not need to know about what's in here," Trixter told Push gravely. "What I've really been doing while you were keeping the sheriff busy was hacking into this thing's computer. According to the readouts I've been getting, this thing has a built-in medical setup."

No one so much as breathed.

"What?" Wiccan Witch asked.

"Are you serious?" Scarlet Queen demanded.

"It can't be," Scratch stated, though he didn't look convinced by his own words. "That thing's not big enough for a full-grown adult to fit in. They'd have to curl up into a ball. It wouldn't leave them room enough to breathe."

"Not a grown adult," Trixter answered heavily. "But there's something alive in this thing. I've been getting readouts for heart rate, breathing, nerve impulses, and brainwave activity. This setup is highly advanced."

"But that doesn't add up," Wiccan Witch protested, scooting forward until she was on the edge of her seat. "Why build something this advanced to monitor and protect something if you were just going to hurl it through space?"

"Assuming it came from space," Wrath added. "Push still thinks this could all be someone's idea of a practical joke."

"I'm slowly turning into a believer," Push said in protest, his eyes locked firmly on the pod. "Can you get it open, Trixter?"

Professor Trixter gave Push an ominous look before pressing something inside the spot where he'd been cutting with his laser torch earlier.

"Done."

A hush swept over the living room. The eyes of everyone present zeroed in on the pod as the front of it split open down the center, then unfolded like the wings of a metal butterfly. A loud, almost painful hiss emerged from it. Inside, Push could make out the sound of something beeping with the regularity of a baby's heartbeat.

A moment later, that thought took on a whole new, more literal meaning.

"Dear Goddess," Wiccan Witch gasped, her eyes doubling in size. "I can't believe it."

"I don't believe it," Scarlet Queen echoed.

"This can't be real," Scratch said softly, leaning in to confirm what he was seeing. "Push, do you see—?"

Push swallowed. His throat had gone dry at some point when the pod opened. The air in the room felt heavy now, as though waiting for thunder to crash.

"I see it," he confessed, while his stomach did jumping jacks. "I see it, Scratch, but I just don't believe it either."

Professor Trixter hadn't moved, hadn't said a word the whole time. Slowly, as if he were sleepwalking, Wrath got up off the couch and knelt down on one knee in front of the pod. He reached in, grasped the sleeping infant with both hands, and carefully lifted him up.

Wires had been stuck to the child's body, presumably for the purpose of monitoring its life signs. A tube was placed down the infant's throat to, Push assumed after a moment of utter horror, feed it. Wrath confirmed this a moment later after removing each wire taped to the baby's azure skin. Slowly, Wrath pulled the tube out, careful not to harm the child.

The beeping from inside the pod, meanwhile, went flat, instead becoming a high-pitched squeal. Professor Trixter flinched at the noise and silenced it at once by slamming his fist down onto the machine, shutting it off.

"Occasionally," he said to a completely disinterested room, "the direct approach works best."

No one cared for the moment. Their attention was still locked on the baby in Wrath's arms. Its skin was the color of lapis stone. A tuft of black hair, as dark as a starless sky, fell in a mess around the child's face and ears. The ears themselves were pointed, though not like an elf's would be from a fantasy story. These looked more like the ears of a cat or a rat.

Despite the differences, the baby was still remarkably human looking overall.

Wrath was holding the child with the utmost care, as if afraid he might drop him. The thought puzzled Push, and he couldn't resist doing a quick check to confirm that the baby was, in fact, male. Because of the shock, he hadn't noticed that the baby was nude or that there ought to have been no mistaking the child's gender.

Wrath stroked the baby's head tenderly, as though he'd done it a thousand times before. The gesture startled Push, and something went through him like a knife to the gut.

The baby's eyes opened at Wrath's touch. Its eyes were yellow, a bright topaz color that didn't belong on any human person. It looked up, locking eyes with Wrath, and smiled.

"Hey, there," Wrath whispered to it in the gentlest voice imaginable. "Welcome to the world, little guy."

"A *BABY*?"

Scarlet Queen's shouting caused the infant to cry out, and she quickly slapped a hand over her mouth.

"Sorry," she uttered around it as the child continued to cry.

Wrath stared at her ruefully for a second before giving the child his full attention. "There, there," Push heard him utter into the baby's fuzz-covered pointy ear. "She didn't mean to scare you. It must be louder out here than you're used to."

Wiccan Witch stood up and edged herself closer to Wrath so she could get a better glimpse. "Can I hold him?" she asked, brushing a finger across the baby's forehead. "Later on, I mean."

It actually looked like Wrath might say no for a moment, but then he nodded.

"This," Push began, louder than he meant to. Quickly, he lowered his voice before speaking again. "This is just...."

"Bizarre," Scratch finished for him. "But sort of cool too, I think."

No one moved, save for Professor Trixter, who stood up to get a closer look at the baby still in Wrath's arms. Wrath jerked away abruptly, as though startled by the movement.

"You're not going to hurt him, are you?" Wrath demanded, almost accusingly.

Professor Trixter gave Wrath a look like he'd lost his mind. "Calm down," he barked, albeit quietly, at Wrath, which caused the baby to let out a brief cry of protest. "I just want to see him."

It looked like Wrath didn't believe him, but Wiccan Witch diffused the situation by placing a hand on Wrath's arm.

"No one's going to hurt him," Scarlet Queen shouted, before remembering to keep her voice down. "We're just... curious, is all."

"Alien babies don't drop out of the sky on us every day," Scratch added for her benefit. "Though, um, I think this answers the question of what those other aliens were doing snooping around the wreckage downtown."

It took a second for Push to catch up with Scratch's train of thought. "The plane," he concluded, once his brain stopped misfiring. "The baby's ship must have hit the tail of the plane. That was what made it crash. And the aliens were digging through the wreckage because they thought the ship had landed there."

Everyone looked up from the child to absorb this. "Why does Sloth want the kid, though?" Scarlet asked, looking around at everyone. "How's he tied up in all of this?"

"A more accurate question," Wrath amended, "would be, 'Why does Sloth's employer want him, and how did they find out about any of this in the first place?'"

Scarlet Queen wasn't offended. "Those are better questions," she said. "I think maybe we should work on figuring that part out."

"And fast," Push agreed. "I'm going to call Sheriff Black again and tell him what you two found at that farmhouse."

Push was looking directly at Wrath and Wiccan Witch now. "It may be a long shot, but it's our only lead at this point. The sooner we find Sloth, the sooner we'll get some answers. At least now the Cape Cabinet can't ignore us anymore."

Scratch laughed, which got everyone save Wrath going. "I guess maybe showing them an alien kid will get their attention," Scratch surmised.

Wrath looked less than happy at the thought. "What will they do with him?" he wondered, speaking to Push specifically. "Are they going to hurt him?"

The thought hadn't even occurred to Push, something he wasn't proud to admit even to himself. Looking around quickly, Push saw that the others were thinking the same thing. Wiccan Witch was the first to step up.

"We won't let anything bad happen," she promised Wrath, giving his arm a squeeze.

It sounded like Wiccan Witch meant every word.

"He's—" Wrath began, only to have his voice crack. "He's just a baby."

"We know."

Scarlet Queen looked across at Wrath as she spoke, and the light in her eyes told Push she was on board with Wiccan Witch. "No one's going to hurt him, Wrath, but we can't keep something this big a secret forever."

Push watched closely as Wrath looked down at the baby in his arms. Slowly, Wrath ran a finger along the baby's forehead, brushing away a lock of hair that hung out of place between the infant's topaz eyes.

"I guess we can't," he said, and Push felt his gut clench at the sorrow in Wrath's voice.

What the hell was wrong with him?

"All the more reason to capture Sloth and get some answers," Scratch said, and then paused to sniff the air gingerly. "What's that smell?"

Wrath's eyes doubled in size. "My soup!" he declared.

Wiccan Witch took the baby from his arms as it was shoved toward her. Wrath took off like a scalded cat for the kitchen. What followed were sounds of him dashing all over the place, banging stuff around while cursing under his breath.

Professor Trixter looked from the kitchen toward the baby, who was staring up at Wiccan Witch curiously, and sighed.

"This kid's been out of that pod for two minutes," he said wearily, "and this place is already going domestic."

"Don't be mean," Wiccan Witch chided, tickling the baby under the chin. "I think he's cute."

"Um, a little I guess," Scratch said, glancing at Push. "What's with you, though? I thought you'd be all over this by now."

Push shifted his feet uncomfortably. "I'm not really wild about kids," he said, and it felt like he was confessing something unpleasant. "They make me nervous."

"He's adorable," Wiccan Witch insisted as Scarlet Queen walked over to see for herself.

"He's pretty weird looking," Scarlet said, peering down at the child. "But I guess that's part and parcel for a space baby. Funny though, he doesn't look anything at all like the aliens you described to us before."

Push frowned suddenly.

"No, he doesn't," Push said, looking over to Scratch. "The ones we fought were more like something out of a B-grade sci-fi flick."

"Um, sort of like walking bugs," Scratch said, nodding thoughtfully. "I think they were kind of blue, though. Maybe that's something?"

Professor Trixter looked away from the girls, who were still engrossed by the space child. "I'm no authority on extraterrestrial life forms," he said, almost apologetically. "My advice would be to ask an expert, but I don't know of one that we can trust with something this big."

"That feels a little odd," Scarlet Queen mused, giving Trixter a thoughtful glance. "I thought the Association had experts in everything by now."

"There was an alien expert Association member," Wiccan Witch exclaimed softly, rising up with a sharp snap. "Ace of Space, he called himself. We used to chat on Skype all the time, back before it got commercial."

Scarlet Queen and Professor Trixter looked hopeful. "He's a friend of yours?" Trixter asked. "Could you contact him?"

Wiccan Witch shook her head sadly in answer before looking back down at the baby, who was waving his arms eagerly up toward her face, trying to get her attention.

"The Cape Cabinet dropped him several years back," she said, playfully tickling the child under the chin. "He was never given a reason why. By that point, I was already on my way to becoming a full-fledged member, and he quit answering my messages. I don't know where he is now."

Wrath stuck his head in through the rear entrance to the kitchen behind Push and Scratch and cleared his throat loudly.

"Soup's ready," he called out. "It's a little overcooked, but I think it will be all right."

"We don't have any baby food, do we?" Wiccan Witch asked before he could duck away.

Wrath froze, along with every other male in the room.

"We don't," Push said.

"Um, it's never occurred to us to buy some," Scratch told her. "We've never had a baby over here before."

"Or anywhere else for that matter," Push added. "Would baby formula kill him?"

"The kid's an alien after all," Scratch pointed out at the shocked looks on everyone else's faces. "We don't know what kind of diet he needs."

"I think I can answer that much," Professor Trixter said abruptly, crouching down beside the pod again. "This thing had some sort of tube built into it that was feeding down his throat. I think the pod was designed to monitor his health and provide nutrition when needed."

"Can you analyze what it was feeding him and replicate it?" Wrath asked excitedly.

Professor Trixter shot him a very dirty glare in response. "I'm not a fucking miracle worker," he snapped. "This stuff came from another planet, supposedly. For all I know, it could be toxic to the rest of us."

Wrath's face became a complete blank. Push felt a chill go through him, like something bad was about to happen.

Wiccan Witch put a hand on Trixter's forearm. "He's a baby," she reminded Trixter, holding him up. "If we don't find some way to feed him, he'll die."

Trixter stared down at the child for a moment, scowling. "I am not changing that kid's diapers," he declared. "Getting me to stare at space baby chow is one thing, but there is no way in hell or on earth that I'm touching alien poop."

"That reminds me," Wiccan Witch replied, turning back to Push and Scratch yet again. "We don't have diapers either, do we?"

Push shook his head while Scratch let out a long sigh.

"I guess we should make a grocery list," Scratch said, speaking to Push specifically. "Let's hope the people in town don't ask too many questions. If they're as nosy and paranoid as Wrath says, this could turn bad real fast."

Push didn't move an inch from his spot. "A baby," he declared, keeping both eyes locked on the child. "Why couldn't the aliens have sent a nice doomsday weapon instead?"

"For all we know, they have," Scarlet Queen pointed out. "For right now, though, the kid seems fairly harmless, so we shouldn't look a gift horse in the mouth."

"We haven't had to burp him yet," said Trixter warningly. "Let's hold off on the 'harmless' assumptions until then."

Wrath's voice echoed through the kitchen, where he'd evidently disappeared to at some point during the conversation.

"The soup is going to get cold!"

Wiccan Witch laughed. "Come on," she said to the baby. "Let's go eat some of Daddy's soup so he'll stop being so cranky."

Scarlet Queen watched her go with eyes as big as saucers. "Now that," she stated flatly, "is just plain creepy."

Push heard Scratch laugh. "No fooling," he agreed, following after them.

The next couple of hours were nothing if not chaotic. Scratch drew the short straw and went out to grab some basic baby supplies while the rest of them put the dishes away. Professor Trixter was able to extract some of the glop that was being fed through the tube in the pod and took a sample to study.

"I don't think he likes it," Wrath noted to Push as Wiccan Witch held a spoon up to the kid's mouth.

"You just have to be patient," she insisted as the child reluctantly covered the spoon with his mouth. "He's not used to eating this way."

Wrath watched the baby eat for a moment as though fascinated by it. Push wasn't entirely sure why he was so fixated on watching the alien baby eat goop from a space pod. Thinking of it in those terms sounded strange, but he couldn't bring himself to pull away. Scarlet Queen was also sitting at the breakfast table in the kitchen, watching the scene with almost rapturous attention.

"What do we call him?" she blurted out unexpectedly.

Wiccan Witch froze in the middle of offering the baby another spoonful. "I don't know," she said, looking from one to the next. "Any ideas?"

"Sorry," Scarlet Queen replied immediately. "I'm not up on my baby names for alien children. I'd end up wanting to call him Han Solo, or maybe Bob."

Push and Wrath locked eyes with each other.

"I vote against Bob," Wrath said dryly.

"Same here," Push agreed. "Any thoughts?"

Wrath stared across the table as Wiccan Witch went back to feeding the kid. Push found himself watching Wrath instead of the baby, entranced by the man's mind at work. He could almost hear Wrath's brain racing at a mile per second.

It suddenly dawned on Push that he was openly staring in front of Scarlet Queen. Just as Push was coming up with an excuse, Wrath spoke.

"Xavier," he said.

Push blinked. "What?"

Wrath cocked an eye at him, which made Scarlet Queen snicker. "He means for the baby's name," she explained, still laughing. "Actually, Xavier's not a bad name, I think."

"I don't know," Wiccan Witch said as the child finished off his meal. "Why Xavier?"

Wrath shrugged. "I always wanted to be called Xavier," he replied quietly. "When I was a kid, I snuck this old X-Men comic into my room. Xavier was a cool name, I thought."

Wiccan Witch shot Wrath an amused glare. "You aren't going to start calling him 'X' for short, are you?" she wondered shrewdly.

"Probably," Wrath replied in a frank tone. "It'll make him a hit with the ladies."

That made Push laugh. "Assuming his species is even into that sort of thing," he pointed out, deliberately watching the kid now.

"It looks like Xavier is his name, then," said Scarlet Queen, satisfied. "Unless someone has a better idea."

"Should we wait until Scratch gets back before deciding anything?" Push asked suddenly. "He and Professor Trixter need a say in this, don't they?"

"Nope," Wiccan Witch declared. "If Trixter won't change diapers, he doesn't get to name the baby. And Scratch will probably think Xavier is a great name. The two of you love X-Men."

"True," Push said, unable to argue. "I guess his name is Xavier."

Unexpectedly, Scarlet Queen started to laugh. "It sounds like we just named a pet," she said, explaining between snickers.

"He isn't a pet," Wrath protested, upset.

"No, Xavier isn't a pet," Wiccan Witch said quickly. "He's family."

The word hit Push, and he felt a curious warmth spread across his chest as baby Xavier locked eyes with him from across the table. The moment was broken when Scratch came staggering through the front door and into the kitchen with arms weighted down by grocery bags.

"You wouldn't believe how expensive all this crap was," he said, tossing everything haphazardly onto the counter. "And that isn't all of it. Someone's going to have to come help me with the rest because this junk is heavy."

"I'll help," Push said, getting up.

"So will I," added Wrath, getting out of his seat after Push. "Keep an eye on him while we're doing that, if you would."

"No problem," Wiccan Witch said sweetly.

"Don't worry, 'Dad,'" Scarlet Queen threw in teasingly. "We won't let anything happen to him."

Scratch followed Push out to the hovercraft, which was parked in the middle of the garage so the side door could open its wingspan without damaging the walls.

"This has been one weird day," Scratch noted as Wrath climbed inside to pass the bags out to the both of them.

"No shit," said Push, taking two from Wrath and handing them along to Scratch. "And it's not over yet. I think our new bundle of joy cinches things. We need to hunt down Sloth and get answers fast before anything else shows up."

Wrath handed the last of the bags to them and hesitated before climbing out. "The farmhouse?" he asked Push.

"Right," Push replied. "I'm going to call Sheriff Black and see if he wants to bring his men along as backup."

Wrath made a face but said nothing.

"We work *with* the police," Scratch reminded Wrath pointedly, stepping back to let the man get out of the hovercraft.

"And besides," Push added, backing Scratch up, "we've tangled with Sloth three times before, and each time, he got away. Extra manpower will come in handy."

"I said nothing," Wrath pointed out, slamming the hovercraft door once they were all clear of it. "You two are in charge. I'm just the guy who goes in to blow stuff up."

Scratch snorted derisively. "Don't try to martyr yourself," he countered in a cool tone. "You're as much a part of this team now as anyone else."

Wrath stopped in his tracks on the way back to the front door. "Really?" he asked, almost insistently. "Then what was I doing fighting the metalsect all by myself today?"

Push opened his mouth to reply and found he had none.

"Most of us don't have superpowers," Scratch answered, as though it should have been obvious. "The cops didn't let us bring our gear when we were all arrested. If we'd taken it with us, they would have confiscated it."

Wrath thought on that for a moment. "Maybe," he decided, turning the doorknob. "I just thought you all wouldn't care if I died."

"Give me a break," Push shouted, startled by his own anger. "What is it with you all of a sudden?"

Wrath didn't answer until after they were all inside. "I don't know," he said finally, keeping his head turned away from Push and Scratch. "Maybe you aren't the only one who gets nervous around kids."

CHAPTER
FOUR

THE REST of the daylight hours were havoc. Two more metalsects appeared to tear downtown apart. Trixter was insisting they use the term, perhaps because of the whole "nanobot" versus "microbot" issue earlier. The first managed to do some serious damage to the local Walmart parking lot before the team arrived to handle the situation. With Trixter's new virus, the machines were deactivated in short order, leaving a giant metallic ant stuck on its back for the cleanup crew to haul away. The crew had actually watched the whole battle take place from a safe distance while drinking soda. One gave Push a wave as they left.

The second one only demolished a couple of the old buildings in the destroyed area of Shove Point. The team was able to respond much faster than before and neutralize the oversized robotic cockroach before it got any farther out of the damage zone.

The team was taking the attacks in shifts. Professor Trixter's theory was that the virus would eventually spread through the microbots' communication network, thereby nullifying the threat they posed. Until then, everyone was tackling the project in teams of three. Push and Scratch were working to make sure each team contained at least one of their heavy hitters. By the end of the day, containing just two of the metalsects had left Push feeling exhausted.

Unfortunately, their job wasn't over. Even Push had to admit that a good night's sleep would suit everyone, considering what their next task was. At last, seemingly by coincidence, they had a solid lead on Sloth's whereabouts. It was too good an opportunity to pass up. Once this was done, Push could look forward to leaving Shove Point and putting the mess of the last couple of weeks behind him. He and

Scratch could go back to Chicago to help the Association get to the bottom of those bombings. The attacks had been weighing on everyone's minds, which was another reason why Push wanted to go ahead and bring the hammer down on Sloth's operation.

Of course, the upcoming assault they were working on with the local authorities was nothing compared to having a baby in the house. Alien or not, the kid was proving to be a handful. Wiccan Witch had taken on the arduous task of being the kid's caregiver while the team was out.

"Let's be pragmatic," she had said when Push asked if she was sure. "I'm not the best fighter of the group. You've got more than enough muscle on the team to handle big bugs and evil supervillains, but none of you have any sort of training with babies."

"And you do?" Scarlet Queen had asked skeptically before softening her tone. "Sorry, that came out wrong. I didn't know you worked with them."

"I was an intern at a hospital," Wiccan Witch had explained while the kid was cooing happily in her arms. "Part of my training was to work in the maternity ward."

Scarlet Queen had flinched at that news.

"Yeah," Wiccan Witch had agreed. "Give me one space baby from another world over a whole room full of screaming human ones."

No one had argued with her afterward.

Between bug battles, Push spent his time on the phone with Sheriff Black and the local state troopers.

"I know organizing a raid on short notice is not something most people consider fun," he said hurriedly to the sheriff, "but we're hoping to get the drop on them before they can move. There's no guarantee Sloth and the others won't have a fallback spot to go to if they suspect we're about to close in."

The sheriff had been quiet while Push was talking, so Push went in for the kill. "Plus," he'd added, "if we can get this mess with Sloth taken care of, most of the Association's business with your town will be done with. After this, there's just the cleanup with those nanobots—"

"Microbots!" Scarlet Queen had shouted from the kitchen.

"Whatever!" he'd called back before giving the sheriff his full attention again. "Once those bugs are shut down for good, we'll be out of your hair."

"You're trying to sell milk to a cow, son," Sheriff Black had replied once he was able to speak. "Nobody wants you outta sight and mind more than me. I'll pull a couple of strings and get the state troopers to help. If you're serious about this, we can close down on the place late tonight."

Hearing Black so cooperative gave Push pause, but he wasn't about to bitch and moan over it now.

"It's done," he'd announced to everyone once Black hung up. "We're going in tonight before Sloth can jump ship."

"I want in," Wrath said at once.

No one looked the least bit shocked by this. "You were already on the list," Push told him, smiling. "Is that a problem for anyone else?"

Unexpectedly, Scratch seemed the most apprehensive. "Um, I'm going to say something," Scratch stated, turning around to look at Wrath squarely.

Wrath waited a moment when Scratch didn't continue. "Go on," he urged. "I have a feeling I know what it is, but continue."

"If there's something you haven't been telling us," Scratch began, looking more reluctant now that he had Wrath and everyone else's attention. "Say it now. I'm not accusing you of anything, but if there's something we need to know, fill us in."

Push waited, but Wrath didn't respond. "You're not going to be thrown out," Scratch went on. "Everybody's made mistakes before, but if there's something you're holding back, speak now."

Finally, Wrath nodded. "I see," he said. "Then I guess there's no point in hiding it anymore."

Everyone in attendance held their breath. Wrath turned toward Wiccan Witch, who was holding the baby in her arms. Wrath gave the two of them an incredibly tender smile.

"It's time you all know the truth," he said, looking away.

"What?" Scarlet Queen wondered, practically on the edge of her seat now.

Wrath let out a deep breath. "I," he began, "love the new *My Little Pony* animated series."

"UM, WHEN did you even have a chance to watch that show?"

Wrath looked back at Scratch's question and frowned.

"Sorry," he replied. "What show?"

Wrath was riding shotgun with Push, whose hands shook as he struggled to bring the hovercraft to a stop.

"Dammit," he swore, forcing the brake down. "This thing is worse than a Mack truck. I don't see how Trixter does it."

With the brake down, the hovercraft rolled to a stop over the grass alongside a row of cop cars. The airbag beneath them promptly deflated, bringing the tanklike vehicle down a couple of feet.

"Sorry about that," Push said, looking around at the other two. "Trixter spent twenty minutes describing what he would do to me if I so much as scuffed his 'precious baby,' so I was doing my best not to ding it. What show were you guys talking about?"

"We weren't," Wrath told him. "And it's no problem. I thought you were doing fine."

"You haven't seen enough of Push's driving," Scratch joked, giving his boyfriend a smile. "I was asking Wrath about when he got the chance to watch *My Little Pony*."

Push turned toward Wrath expectantly. "I was curious about that myself," he admitted. "When did you watch that show?"

"It's no big deal," Wrath said dismissively. "Wiccan Witch pointed me to this site a few nights back where someone had uploaded the whole series. It took about six episodes, but she got me hooked."

"Professor Trixter watches it," Scratch told him seriously. "You two should schedule a marathon soon."

"Great," Push muttered, opening his door. "A house half full of bronies. I think I'd rather go fight supervillains and monstrous robots now."

Wrath climbed out next, followed by Scratch. The area was congested with state patrol troopers and members of the Shove Point police department. Everyone was watching the threesome closely, looking less than pleased. A few eyes would give the hovercraft appreciative, almost envious glances every so often, but the air was still choked with ire.

"When I was a child," Wrath said unexpectedly, flames dancing in the palms of his hands, "a boy would just as soon fall on something rusty and sharp than admit he watched a show like *My Little Pony.*"

"The world is a strange place sometimes," Push said.

Wrath shot him a smirk. "I believe the three of us are living proof of that."

Scratch was watching the fire in Wrath's hands wave eagerly. "Um, you might want to tone it down some," he advised, noting the added tension on the cops' faces now. "I don't think the pyrotechnics are making anyone here more comfortable."

Wrath took in a deep breath and clenched his hands into tight fists, extinguishing the flames.

"Everything okay?" Push wondered.

"It's the emotions from everyone here," Wrath explained, looking around carefully. "In case you hadn't noticed, the people here aren't happy to see us."

Push followed the path of Wrath's gaze and spotted Sheriff Black off in the distance. The sheriff was having a conversation with a state trooper sergeant. Whatever the two were saying, the sergeant looked less than pleased about it.

"Can you get anything off the two of them?" Push asked Wrath in a hushed voice, nodding toward the sheriff and sergeant.

Wrath looked both men up and down and narrowed his eyes. A look of concentration twisted his face for a moment.

"My guess," Wrath said, still focused on the two, "is that they're arguing about us. It feels as though the sheriff might be arguing in our favor. The sergeant is really upset about something, and my hunch says it's us."

"The sheriff is arguing in our favor?" Scratch wasn't trying to hide the skepticism in his voice. "Um, are you sure?"

"Reasonably sure," Wrath said. "It's just a theory, but I suspect the sheriff is going along with us so we'll get out of his town faster."

"That makes sense," Push acknowledged after a moment. "If we leave, Shove Point goes back to normal, and Black won't have to worry anymore."

"The sergeant hasn't had to deal with the same problems Black has over the last few days," Wrath concluded. "He's not too keen on letting costumed weirdos mess up his raid."

Scratch frowned. "We're still within Shove Point's city limits, right?" he asked, looking to Push for confirmation. "This makes it the sheriff's party."

"We are," Wrath confirmed. "But tell that to the other guy."

The farmhouse was in the distance. None of the cops were running their strobes. Someone gave the word, and the local yokels began moving forward. Instead of following along, Black made his way over to where the trio stood.

"They're about to surround the place," he said, filling them in. "The state sergeant wanted to secure the area before anyone goes inside."

"So who is going inside?" Scratch asked carefully.

Black sighed. "You boys don't make it easy for me, you know that?" the sheriff moaned as though whatever weighed on his mind was their fault. "The sergeant wanted to handle this himself, but this is still in my yard. He wasn't wild about sending the three of you in, and neither am I, but you fellas have the most experience in dealing with this nut. Once the perimeter is secure, assuming you can handle this, the three of you will make your way inside."

Black passed a walkie-talkie to Push. "Need help," he said, "don't hesitate to radio for backup."

Push clipped the communicator to his belt. "We got it," he assured the sheriff, whose eyes suddenly narrowed in confusion.

"Where's the rest of your outfit?" he asked, frowning. "I figured the whole show would be here for this."

"Wiccan Witch is on monitor duty," Push said quickly, hoping the sheriff didn't notice the abrupt twitch his body made. "Professor Trixter and Scarlet Queen stayed behind in case we have any more metalsect attacks."

It was mostly true. Wiccan Witch was actually abstaining from the fight to babysit, but Push wasn't ready to let the sheriff in on that secret, especially not with so many other cops in the vicinity. If there was trouble, Wiccan Witch was supposed to alert them, so in all technicality, Push hadn't been lying.

"You're not worried about two of your people tackling big metal bugs all by their lonesome?" Black asked, bringing Push back to the situation at hand.

"Scarlet Queen and Trixter can take care of themselves," Scratch assured Black. "With Trixter's virus, the bugs shut down pretty fast."

"It looks like they're about ready," Wrath interrupted, looking off in the distance.

"You're right." Push took a deep breath to steady himself. "Let's go, boys."

Push kept reminding himself as the three of them moved across the dark farm property that it was a very simple operation. Sloth and his company weren't expecting any attacks. Wrath's stumbling on their hideout was nothing but serendipity moving in their favor for once. Push had no reason at all by this point to doubt the man's loyalty. He'd seen Wrath fight before.

There was nothing for him to be worried about.

Push glanced at Wrath as they approached the dark farmhouse and felt his heart race. Wrath was moving across the ground like a cat, only much larger and far more dangerous. Things inside Push's body clenched, against his better judgment.

Looking away, Push focused on Scratch, who was moving along at a slightly slower pace on Push's right. The ache inside Push's chest eased ever so slightly at the sight of his boyfriend. Scratch and he were in a relationship now. Scratch wanted to be with Push and no one else. Furthermore, Push wanted to be with Scratch. He'd wanted that for years and never expected it to happen.

So why was he letting himself get torn up over his relationship and whatever Wrath was doing to him when there was a job to be done?

Push gritted his teeth and forced his brain to focus on the task at hand. There would be time for romantic entanglements later. In fact, Push decided as they reached the farmhouse back wall, there was nothing here to work out. He loved Scratch with all his heart and soul. There was nothing more to work out between them.

Wrath's fingers accidentally brushed Push's as they pressed their backs against the half-rotted wooden structure. Something pulsed below Push's belt, and he was very grateful at that moment that it was so dark. Unfortunately, despite his previous protesting, the relief had nothing to do with the fact that they were about to attack a house containing at least three supervillains.

"Everything cool?" Scratch asked.

"Yeah," Push said, sounding out of breath as he swept the region with the night vision mode on his goggles. "The coast is still clear."

"Um, I meant with you," Scratch clarified. "You seem tenser than usual."

"I'm fine," said Push, forcing calm through his body as Scratch moved a little closer to him. Their bodies weren't touching, but having Scratch so close caused almost every muscle in Push's body to relax some.

"Thanks," he said without thinking.

Scratch frowned. "For what?"

That made Push chuckle softly. "Nothing," he insisted. "I'll have to tell you about it some other time."

"Hey, lovebirds," Wrath interjected quietly.

Push jerked around and saw that Wrath had moved several feet away toward a window. Soft light was coming through it, though not enough to disrupt Push's night vision.

"We've got a problem," Wrath went on.

"What?" Scratch asked. "Have you spotted them?"

Push hesitated, then eased down the wall toward Wrath. "More than that," Wrath said as Scratch followed along behind Push. "Sloth invited some new people to the party."

That got Push to stop short. "Who?" he wondered, even though the answer was already pretty clear.

"Gluttony and Greed."

Scratch placed a hand on Push's shoulder, leaning into him, and let out a low growl of frustration.

"Terrific," he said. "I guess that means the whole gang is coming to town. Any chance you knew about this?"

Wrath shook his head. "Sorry," he answered apologetically. "I told you everything that Sloth told me when he arranged for that meeting at the arcade. He hinted that something big was going down, but I didn't expect Gluttony or Greed to show up here."

Push eased farther down toward Wrath and peeked through the window. "Which is which?" he asked, glancing back and forth at the two women sitting side by side at a dusty old table. One had peach skin and dirty-blonde hair cut in a vaguely Jennifer Aniston style, and was lithe like a cat. The other was ever so slightly more muscular, with skin as dark as her companion's was light. A knotted braid trailed down the back of her chair.

"Gluttony is the one with the cane," Wrath answered as Scratch joined them, pointing to the black woman. "She's been blind since she was a little girl. Greed is the one wearing the rubber gloves."

"And their powers?"

"I really need to get you to sit down and read the Deadly Seven's dossier," Scratch told Push after he was done chuckling quietly.

"Keep it down," Wrath ordered them. "Gluttony has enhanced hearing and spatial awareness. Her entire body is basically one big receiver."

"What about Greed?" Push asked absentmindedly, keeping his eyes focused on the scene unfolding through the dirty window.

"Her body's a living Taser weapon," Scratch answered quickly under his breath. "Um, wait a sec, though. If Gluttony has super-Daredevil powers, does that mean she knows we're out here?"

Push's eyes widened as Gluttony raised an arm behind her. In it was what looked like a loaded .38 Special. Without turning around in her seat, she fired through the window, riddling it with bullets.

Push had already dragged both men to the ground with him. The glass above them shattered, raining down like sharp pellets.

"She saw us," Wrath confirmed, rising up just far enough so they could hear him. "It seems she hasn't lost her temperament, either."

"I heard that!"

The shout came from inside the house. Push rolled out from under Scratch in time to see Gluttony stick her head out through the shattered window. Her head was positioned perfectly to avoid the few hanging shards that were left. Though her head was tilted the wrong way slightly, there was no doubt in Push's mind that the woman knew their position.

Push's hands were dangerously close to getting shredded by the window shards lurking in the grass. Wrath, meanwhile, stood up and looked at Gluttony directly. Behind Gluttony stood Greed, whose eyes widened in surprise.

"Wrath?" Greed asked happily. "I'd heard you were let out, but I didn't think you were here."

"Hello, Greed."

Push heard Wrath greet her warmly, like a long-lost family member, and something inside his gut sank.

"Not instilling a lot of confidence in your teammates right now, Wrath," he grunted, getting up off the ground carefully.

Push saw Wrath roll his eyes as he and Scratch helped one another up. "Boy, what'chu doin' here?" Gluttony demanded in a distinctly Southern drawl.

Now that he was standing, Push could spot Sloth in the background, holding up a very large assault gun.

"If he's smart," Sloth warned, aiming for Push's head, "he's here to get with the program."

In response, Gluttony fired her gun behind her, shooting Sloth's gun out of his hand. The albino muscle man cried out in pain. Greed watched him stagger for a moment, then turned back to face Wrath.

"Please tell me you're not here to sign up with this loser again?" she asked, almost pleadingly. "We were all younger and stupider the last time."

"I'm not," Wrath assured her. "I was hoping I could say the same for you two."

Gluttony snorted. "We're troubleshooters for a security firm now," she explained. "The company we work for said they had some big shot client wantin' both a' us to test their newfangled security system."

"Only the client turns out to be this idiot," Greed finished, rolling her eyes. "We almost left right then and there, but he promised us ten grand off the top if we listened to his proposal."

"What can we say?" Gluttony jumped in, shrugging. "Money's been tight, and it wasn't like either of us were actually gonna say yes to him."

Wrath smiled, and the almost childlike joy on his face was enough to make Push pause. Scratch didn't suffer from the same problem, however.

"This is all very touching," said Scratch, stepping forward between them. "I'm really glad you two aren't planning to put our heads on a platter, but I think the bad guy is getting away."

Sloth had broken into a run while the others were talking. Push looked past Greed and Gluttony in time to see the charging behemoth crash through a wall and roll to a stop in the next room.

"Not for long," Wrath said, unfazed, summoning fire to his hands. "The whole property is surrounded. He can't get far."

"Want some help?" Gluttony asked, giving her gun a practiced twirl. "I was gonna check to see if anybody had a reward out on the dang fucker."

"Sure," replied Wrath, grinning from ear to ear now. "It'll be just like old times."

Then he looked at Push and Scratch, as though remembering the two were there. "Except we can't kill him," Wrath added. "That's out."

Scratch leaped through the window, missing the glass completely, and charged past Greed and Gluttony.

"Bad guy," he shouted back at them. "Still getting away. Go around and take the other side."

Sloth was indeed working his way through the rest of the house, not even stopping for walls that were blocking his path.

"We're with the cute one," Greed said, breaking into a run after Scratch alongside Gluttony. "You two slowpokes cut him off."

Wrath seized Push by the forearm and took off, dragging him along behind. "I can run by myself," Push growled, jerking his arm away.

"Then move," Wrath snapped back. "We get Sloth, and half of our mission is over. Then you and Scratch can go back to Shy Town and get me out of your lives for good."

Both men were pouring on the steam as they heard Sloth crash through the far outer wall on the other end of the farmhouse. Gunfire followed, undoubtedly from Gluttony's handguns.

"What?" Push demanded, reminding himself not to get distracted and slow down. "Who said I wanted you out of the way?"

"Don't you?"

The conversation came to an abrupt close as they rounded the corner of the half-standing structure together. Scratch was holding back Sloth using his cue stick. The laser built into the tip was firing at full blast, burning away at the surface of Sloth's dense skin. Gluttony was firing as well, each shot striking dead-on. Despite this, the bullets did little more than annoy the pale-skinned muscle monstrosity.

"No more kid gloves," Greed yelled over the din, stripping off the rubber gloves concealing her hands. "I've waited years to do this."

Push thrust his palm out and blasted Sloth with a telekinetic pulse. The man mountain barely registered the pain from it, but it was enough to earn Push his full attention. That turned out to be all Greed needed. As Sloth gave his back to her, Greed charged forward and leaped onto his shoulders. As their bodies connected, her bare hands slammed down onto each side of Sloth's thick neck.

Something that sounded like bacon frying filled the air along with the distinctive stench of human flesh being burned. Sloth's eyes bulged out from their sockets as his body convulsed.

"Living Taser weapon," Wrath reminded, looking toward Push. "If you don't mind, though, I'll avoid making the clichéd 'shocking' pun."

"Thank you," said Push, sending another bolt at Sloth's midsection, aiming as far from Greed as he could.

Greed rolled off onto the grass when the telekinetic bubble connected. Gluttony took point from several feet back and held Sloth's attention while Scratch tossed up several billiard balls. With Greed now out of the way, Wrath let loose with the fire, pouring flames all over Sloth's body until his clothes were nothing but smoldering ruins. Sloth roared, hurt and angry, but got cut off as several of Gluttony's shots struck him upside the temple. Blood poured from these wounds, but it still wasn't enough to put him down.

"Triple shot," Scratch called out, taking aim. "Keep clear."

Greed flipped back out of the way as all three balls connected. Push recognized them as the special polymer adhesive type. Each one shattered on impact, spreading glue all over Sloth's body. In seconds, he was covered from head to toe in the stuff, unable to move.

"Better than a straitjacket," Scratch said, smirking to himself.

"Nice job," Greed said, laughing.

"Are we clear?" Gluttony asked, keeping her guns at the ready.

"We're clear," Greed assured her, giving Sloth a wide berth as she made her way around to where Gluttony stood. "You were awesome, lover."

Push blinked but turned away as the two ladies kissed. From the sound of things, the local authorities were coming their way.

"Nice of them to show up finally," Wrath said disdainfully.

Sloth grunted in frustration, unable to move his sealed jaw, as what might as well have been a platoon of local cops and state troopers closed in on their position.

"Guess we'd better go," Greed said, disengaging from Gluttony's mouth. "It was good seeing you again, Wrath. You should come by and visit us in Paris now that you're out and about."

"I'll ask my parole officers later," he replied, giving Scratch and Push a look each.

"I thought they were supposed to give a signal," the state trooper sergeant yelled as he and Sheriff Black reached them.

"Must've slipped their minds," Black replied, though he looked oddly satisfied by the sergeant's scowl.

Greed and Gluttony were hanging back close to the shadows, out of sight. Neither one of them had made a move yet to take their leave. Evidently, they were waiting for the right moment when the attention was less focused on them. Wrath kept glancing their way, as though saddened now.

"Don't worry," Push whispered to him. "We're not going to blow the whistle on them. They helped us capture Sloth. That counts for a lot."

"Yeah," Scratch agreed, standing alongside his boyfriend. "Um, I think we can work something out."

Push snickered. "Actually," he said, "given the way the Cape Cabinet have been ignoring my reports, we could just neglect to mention they were even here. They might not notice if we told them Greed and Gluttony showed up riding on flying saucers."

Scratch found that funny, but Wrath looked less than pleased. "Let's not joke about flying saucers right now," he said, keeping back away from the crowd of officers that were congregating around a still-unmoving Sloth.

"What?" Scratch's face lit up as he realized what Wrath meant. "Oh, right."

All three of them watched as Sloth fought against the glue that was holding his legs together and pinning both arms to his sides.

"I can't believe it's finally over," Wrath said softly.

Push opened his mouth but was cut off by a loud roar. "Roar" was the best way his brain could describe it. As the sound was emitted again somewhere high overhead, he reasoned briefly that it was more like a car horn mixed with a washboard being scraped while a mother elephant gave birth. The noise was horrible and eerily unfamiliar.

Almost... *alien.*

Push stared up into the sky. The others, all of them, did the same. The gasps that came from there sounded dim in Push's ears. There was nothing from him. His body was too fixed on what was happening overhead to worry about reacting.

There were at least a dozen of them, maybe more, and every last one was converging on the small town of Shove Point. Unlike the old films, none of the ships were flat and circular. These things reminded

Push of wasps' nests or beehives. There was something vaguely insectoid about their appearance.

Each ship passed over the town once, twice, and a third time in a zigzagging formation. Now that they were closer, Push could do a count. There was a total of fifteen ships in the fleet. The ships looked small, bigger than an aircraft but not too terribly much more. Something was being dropped out of them each time a ship passed over the outskirts of town. One ship roared past them overhead and left a deposit several feet farther back from where they stood.

Push saw that it was some sort of receiver antenna. When the device landed, it began imbedding itself in the ground. As the dust around it settled, the upper half of the device extended higher, stretching itself out like a child's toy might transform. Then the tip lit up, and a bright flash blinded them all.

When Push could see again, the sky was being engulfed by some sort of sick green glow. The same light was coming from the tower behind them and across town in other places where the machines had been left.

"What is it?" Gluttony asked quietly, fearful. "The hell-ass is goin' on?"

"It's a force field, baby," Greed whispered back. "The whole town's being sealed off from the outside."

"What?" Gluttony sounded angry now rather than frightened. "By what?"

"By aliens," Push said. "We're being invaded."

Every eye that wasn't Wrath or Scratch zeroed in on Push. "This isn't over," Wrath said. "This is just the beginning."

CHAPTER FIVE

"SAY THAT again?"

Gluttony grabbed hold of Greed's hand and clutched at it tightly. "Sweetie pie, this here's a lousy time for you t' decide to punk your girlfriend."

"She isn't," Wrath said, keeping his eyes glued to the skies. "Aliens have landed in Shove Point and sealed the town off using a force field."

Wrath paused, looking back down toward Push, and frowned. "I guess when you say it out loud, it does sound pretty far-fetched," he mused.

Push looked away from Wrath toward the city. Lights were going out one after the other, and they could hear the stirrings of what Push felt for certain was the beginnings of a full-blown panic.

It was hero time.

"We need to get down there," he said, loud enough for everyone to hear. "Those people are going to panic soon, and when people panic, it's always bad."

The state trooper sergeant gave him a nasty glare. "Who died and made you king, sonny?" the older man demanded in a much louder voice.

Scratch gripped Push's shoulder, silencing him before he could speak, and stepped up. "Do you want to sit around on your fat asses and decide who gets to be in charge," he said in a low, almost threatening voice, "or do you want to do your jobs?"

"Against aliens?" one trooper off to the side asked. "Have you lost your marbles? None of us are getting paid nearly enough for this shit."

"Then stay behind," Push said. "We'll handle it if we have to. Anyone who wants to come, get in your vehicles and get downtown. We need to stop this before it catches wind and gets too big for all of us."

"And the saucer people?"

This question came from Deputy McGee. Until now, Push hadn't noticed him in the crowd. He'd been conspicuously absent when Push had arrived with the others.

"One problem at a time," Push replied, keeping his cool. "First we keep the local citizens from making the problem worse, and then we worry about the uninvited guests."

Flames danced in Wrath's hands again. "Fine by me," he said, juggling small fireballs. "I've got something to check on while I'm down there anyway."

Push didn't have to guess what Wrath was referring to.

"You two ladies want to join us?" Wrath asked, speaking to Greed and Gluttony. "There's plenty of fun for everyone."

Greed and Gluttony glanced at each other, but it was Gluttony who looked the most eager. "Sure," she said, giving both guns a twirl. "When are we going to get to fight real aliens again?"

Scratch laughed. "I like them," he said, smirking.

"The others will already be working on the situation," Push said. "Let's hurry."

Push was surprised he hadn't had fifteen different messages from Trixter, Scarlet Queen, and Wiccan Witch already. He, Scratch, and Wrath piled into the hovercraft along with Greed and Gluttony. As he started the engines, Push caught sight of Gluttony giving Wrath a hug from behind.

"It's good to see you again, babycakes," Push heard her say.

"Likewise, Gluttony," Wrath replied warmly.

This earned him a smack upside the head from her. "Don't call me 'Gluttony,'" she snapped, though not as harshly as Push had expected. "I haven't been 'Gluttony' in years, and it was a stupid code name anyway. It's Marquita now, okay?"

"Fine," Wrath said, nursing his sore head. "But did you have to hit me so hard?"

"It'll help you remember," replied Marquita, sitting back down next to Greed.

"It's Rachel," she said, looking past Wrath at Push and Scratch. "'Greed' was something I did a long time ago and nothing I brag about these days."

Push nodded at their reflections through the rearview mirror and took off down the road. Being a hovercraft, the vehicle was far more adept at traveling cross-country than police cars. Push saw no reason not to take advantage of this and tore over the country path leading down toward town.

"Don't tell Professor Trixter we came home this way," Push asked Scratch as they hit an especially hard bump.

"Won't say a word," Scratch replied, trying to reach someone at the house on his own cell phone.

"It'd be mine against yours anyway," Wrath chimed in from behind.

"Thanks, Wrath," Push told him, before giving the path his full attention.

Marquita groaned. "Don't tell me this fool is still callin' hisself 'Wrath,'" she said angrily. "What the hell is the matter with you?"

"It's a cool name," Wrath insisted.

"What's wrong with 'John'?" Rachel wondered, which resulted in her getting a very stern look from Wrath.

"John was my father's name," he answered resolutely. "I'm Wrath."

"Dammit!" Scratch's curse cut through the moment the three were having and made Push snap his attention back to the path they were on.

"Shit!" he screamed, turning the hovercraft sharply to the left in order to avoid slamming into a tree line. "Sorry," he apologized.

"Are you tryin' to get us all killed before the bug-eyed aliens can have a chance?" Marquita wondered, straightening her dark shades as she rose off Rachel's lap.

"Push doesn't handle off-road so well," Wrath told her.

"I said I was sorry," he muttered, keeping both eyes on the road now. "What was the problem, Scratch?"

"I've been trying to get in touch with someone at the house," Scratch said, glaring at his phone as if it were the machine's fault. "They may have already left to try and curtail some of the panic, and we need to touch base with each other to compare notes."

"Maybe the aliens are jamming the signal," Rachel suggested. "That's how it always happens in the movies."

"It doesn't matter," Push said as the hovercraft rolled over a sidewalk into a city street. "We're back in town. Wrath, care to navigate for me?"

People were coming out of their homes now. Push had been expecting looters and hordes of terrified locals, but it seemed that the general populace was only just now beginning to realize what was going on.

Getting an idea, Push reached down to turn on the radio as he guided the hovercraft through the streets around pedestrians.

"Radio signal's a no-go," he said. "That means all transmissions coming into the city from outside may have been cut off. It looks like you were right, Rachel."

"Figures," Wrath grumbled disdainfully. "Aliens invade, and the only way any of these morons notices is because the cable went out. We'll be lucky if some drunk rednecks don't try to storm those ships themselves."

Rachel was giving Wrath a very odd look. "I'd forgotten how much you hated your hometown," she said in a somewhat awestruck tone.

"So he was always like this?" Scratch inquired, looking back as Push spotted a straight track of road ahead with no one milling around in the streets. Pressing his foot down on the gas, Push revved the engine and took off, giving his boyfriend a slight case of whiplash in the process.

"Sorry," Push apologized.

"I hope we get home soon," Wrath commented. "Otherwise, Push really is going to kill us before the aliens can."

Push shot Wrath the bird before gripping the steering wheel. "That doesn't seem very heroic," he overheard Wrath tell Marquita and Rachel.

They reached the house a few minutes later. Scarlet Queen, Wiccan Witch, and Professor Trixter were all standing outside in the darkened driveway looking up at the sky. A fourth, much shorter figure was also with them, but Push barely registered the fact. Push pulled the hovercraft up along the side of the road in the path of the driveway; then he and the others quickly disembarked.

"We thought you were never going to get here," Trixter said, then turned to his precious hovercraft. "Please tell me those aren't tree branches!"

"Um, how long have you guys been waiting?" Scratch asked, diverting attention away from Push.

"A few minutes," said Wiccan Witch. "We were hoping you would call."

"How's—" Wrath began, cutting himself off when he noticed the young girl standing near Scarlet Queen.

"Fine," Wiccan Witch answered. "This is Sally, by the way. She says her dad is the one you rented the house from."

Now Push recognized her. "Sorry for intruding," Sally apologized, lowering her head for good measure in the process. "My parents weren't home, and I got a little scared."

Scarlet Queen rubbed the back of the girl's head reassuringly. "This would be the time for it," Scarlet told the girl.

"We tried to call," Scratch said, "but the aliens must be blocking communication signals."

"That explains why the cable's out," Scarlet Queen mused quietly, moving her hand away from Sally's head.

"The net's down too," Professor Trixter said. "Which means getting help from the outside is out. There's no phones, no land lines, no e-mail…."

Trixter paused. "And who are they?" he asked, pointing at Rachel and Marquita.

"Rachel and Marquita," Push said.

"Formerly known as Greed and Gluttony of the Deadly Seven," Scratch went on.

"Sloth tricked them into coming here thinking they would sign on with him," said Push.

"They helped us bag the guy," finished Scratch. "He should be in police custody, assuming none of the local cops left him there at that farmhouse."

"Oh Lord and Lady," Wrath moaned, looking around at Marquita and Rachel. "They're doing that annoying couples thing where they finish each other's sentences."

Marquita grinned and patted Rachel on the arm. "At least they aren't flirting," Rachel pointed out, though she was giving Marquita a knowing look the whole time.

The others were too busy staring to trade further quips with Wrath over Push and Scratch's behavior.

"Okay," Trixter said cautiously. "So why are they here?"

Scratch answered by pointing up at the sky. "Um, to help us fight bad guys and aliens," he said, like it was obvious.

"You think you can handle aliens all by yer lonesome?" Marquita challenged, holding up her guns.

"Down, girl," Rachel warned gently. "Save it for the space freaks."

"We need any help we can get," Push insisted. "So let's not waste time talking. Or flirting, for that matter. Now that we're all together, we need to form a plan."

Professor Trixter sighed. "I suppose this means I'll be stuck building gear for those two while you guys get to fend off alien invaders, huh?"

"We'll need it," Scratch told him. "I counted over a dozen ships when they flew over the town."

"Then let's not waste time," Wrath said. "I can sense it in the air. These people are getting ready to cut loose."

WICCAN WITCH found a neighbor for Sally to stay with, then returned to stand guard at the house while the others walked the streets. Push felt sick with worry at the thought of leaving her behind. He'd forced himself not to think about it, but the evidence was too overwhelming. The longer he spent on the streets, the more convinced he was that the aliens were looking for the space baby hidden at their house. That was the most likely reason for the town being invaded.

Or it would have been if there were any actual aliens wandering around. The streets were filled with people, but none of them extraterrestrials, at least not as far as Push could tell. The police and state troopers trapped inside the force field were doing their best to keep everyone calm. None of the locals looked happy to see the Association. In the end, Push started to think they were making things worse.

"Let's head home," Push said, following a nasty disagreement with one drunken man who was now struggling to get out of the bushes he'd landed in.

"That wasn't like you," Scratch said, staring at the spot where Push had telekinetically thrown the drunkard.

"I know," Push admitted. "But we've got bigger problems. Since the cops seem to have the situation under control for now…"

"And the locals look ready to rip us apart?" Scratch offered.

"That too. I think we should go back to headquarters. We've got some serious thinking to do before the shit hits the fan."

All around them, the sounds of the city echoed through buildings and treetops. The silence that had stunned the city was crumbling now. People weren't quite approaching riot levels of panic yet, but the noise gave Push the impression it wouldn't take much more to set everyone off. People were shouting over air raid and police sirens, running their vehicles trying to look for a way out, and ringing church bells. It was the most clamor Push had ever heard from Shove Point.

"And I've got a feeling I know about what," Scratch told Push, snapping him out of his thoughts as they broke into a run together. "The question is, what do we do about this?"

Push knew Scratch was going to ask him that and hated the fact. "Alien spaceship hits puddle-jumper plane, which crashes into small town, while said spaceship lands in the woods. Then giant robots attack us, followed by more aliens landing and sealing off the town."

"I get it," Scratch huffed. "Um, it doesn't take a Trixter to realize what's going on. More than likely, our friendly neighborhood Shi-ar ambassadors are looking for the little bundle of joy we've got tucked away at our house."

"And for all we know," Push continued, keeping pace with his lover, "the aliens have every right to him."

"Um, about that part." Scratch paused as they rounded a corner and veered off to the side to avoid hitting a family praying together in a circle. "If the kid belongs to these guys, and they're the same ones that were snooping through the plane wreckage, how come they don't look like the baby?"

Push and Scratch split apart momentarily as a police car came down the street toward them. "That is a good point," he agreed once they were at each other's sides again. "So maybe these aliens are cut from a different mold?"

"Too soon to tell." Scratch nodded up ahead at an approaching figure that Push recognized as Wrath. "So far, we haven't seen any other aliens to compare."

Wrath slowed to a stop and turned around as Push and Scratch caught up with him. "Thank Goddess I found you two," he gasped.

It sounded as though he'd been running for quite a ways. "There's trouble," Wrath went on, racing in step with them. "With communication shut down, I thought I was going to have to tackle it all by myself."

"Aliens?" Push and Scratch asked together.

Wrath shook his head. "Not aliens," he said. "More metalsects, or whatever the hell you want to call the sons of bitches."

"Shit!" Push exclaimed. "I'd completely forgotten about those."

"Me too," Scratch said, turning to Wrath. "Where?"

"Just up ahead," Wrath answered, pointing.

With all the noise, it was little wonder they didn't hear the metalsects attacking first. Once Wrath pointed it out, though, Push's ears tuned in and picked up the noises of metal hammering into concrete and people crying out.

"Motherfucker!" Scratch snarled once they reached a new street with haphazardly placed houses on both sides.

There were three of them, and each one was as big as a tank. One resembled an armored beetle; it was the one in front. The second was some sort of fly with rotor blades where the wings should have been. Push couldn't place what sort of species the robot was trying to emulate, assuming it was trying at all. The last one was a spider. All three were marching down the street, turning every few steps as though searching for something.

"Do those things look lost?" Scratch asked.

"Maybe," Push said, thinking. "Why haven't they attacked anyone or knocked over any cars yet? The last metalsect tried to rip apart a busy street."

"They aren't lost," Wrath said, following the robotic creatures movements through squinted eyes. "It looks like they're searching for something."

"Um, what would they want from this place?" Scratch wondered, not leaving Push's side. "The metalsects were made from nanobots—"

"Microbots," Wrath corrected.

"Not now," Push chided, giving Wrath a smack across the side.

"From microbots that were stolen from one of the Association's tech warehouses," Scratch went on. "I thought Sloth programmed these to trash the town so we'd be too busy to look for him."

"Unless the aliens reprogrammed them," Push said abruptly, alarmed.

Scratch glared at Push out the corner of one eye. "I'm hoping you're wrong," he said grimly, "because I do not want to spend the whole night fighting off alien-possessed robotic insects."

"How would the aliens know about the microbots in the first place?" Wrath asked.

"Don't know," Push said.

The metalsects had nearly reached them now.

"But we're going to have to do something about them," Push continued. "Even though it's just the three of us."

"I just had a thought," Wrath said, looking around at the part of town they were in. "Did anyone besides me notice that this neighborhood connects to the one we're staying in?"

Push had a sudden sick feeling in his stomach.

"I think your theory about the aliens controlling the microbots has merit," Wrath said, his mouth stretching thinly. "I also think we know what these things are looking for now."

"Take them down one at a time," Push ordered. "Try not to let them spread us apart, and don't get killed."

"That last part was on my to-do list anyway," Scratch joked, whipping out his cue stick.

"No dying," Wrath noted dryly, summoning fire into his hands. "Must remember not to forget that one."

All three of them made tracks for the spider. Of the three, it was the largest and somehow most intimidating of all three metalsects.

"Take out the legs," Wrath called out, aiming for the two in back.

"We know already," Scratch retorted as a laser blast from the end of his cue stick struck the spider's third leg from the front on the joint.

Push said nothing, blasting the remaining legs with bolt after bolt of telekinetic force. Scratch launched a trick ball into the air, sending it ricocheting off each leg. The ball opened up to unfurl a bolo, which tied two legs together. The spider came crashing down a moment later. The three men backed as far away as they could before the behemoth slammed into the ground.

Wrath pumped flames through his hands at the metal beast, setting it ablaze. "No reason we shouldn't be thorough," he explained when Push and Scratch looked on in surprise.

"Um, that's not thorough," Scratch replied. "That's overkill."

Strangely, the two remaining metalsects hadn't paid them any attention. Both were still moving down the road closer and closer toward what Push suspected was their target.

"Fly or beetle?" Scratch asked.

"Fly," Wrath voted. "Take out its rotors and there's no air support."

"Assuming it flies at all," Push said, thinking out loud. "So far, the thing's stayed grounded."

"Be grateful for small favors," Scratch pointed out. "This thing would be a hell of a lot harder if it were already in the air."

Scratch reached into his coat pocket as they crept up behind the marching mechanical fly. Four balls went sailing into the air, only to be caught one at a time in Scratch's left hand.

"Watch this," he said. "Break!"

One after the other, Scratch launched each ball in an arc through the air. All four landed inside the rotors.

"Glue bombs," Scratch explained, "and bolos. Had to use all of them, but that thing won't be going anywhere now."

"Can you break it open?" Wrath asked Push.

Push got a running start and climbed on the back of the mechanical fly. Wrath followed right after and shielded his face as Push summoned a small telekinetic bomb in his hands.

"You're getting better at making those," Wrath noticed. "I know now isn't the time, but are you aware that you don't seem to be having the same issues with your powers that you did before?"

Push jerked his head toward Wrath, who was helping himself up onto top of the bug. "Empath, remember?" Wrath reminded. "You were wound way tighter when we first met."

Push shook off Wrath's comments and tossed the telekinetic bomb down into a ventilation port on the fly's back. As both of them fell back, Push made a mental note to think over what Wrath had to say later on.

The telekinetic bomb went off right after he thought this, blowing a hole down to the machine's inner workings.

"I don't have a witty comment for this one," Wrath said, moving over to it.

"Something about heartburn?" Push recommended as Wrath fried the mechanical fly's insides with his flame powers. "Or indigestion?"

"Too clichéd," Wrath said. "Also, we probably want to get off this thing now."

Push didn't bother asking why. The two of them leaped off the fly's back and ran for cover, taking Scratch with them. Before they were completely clear, the fly exploded, sending out a shockwave of kinetic force and noise that knocked all three down.

"I spotted what looked like a gas tank inside that thing," Wrath explained, helping the two up once he was on his feet.

"Good eyes," Scratch moaned, taking a deep breath as he stood up. "Now there's just the beetle left."

"And I think the explosion got its attention," Push warned, letting go of Wrath's hand quickly once he was back on his feet.

Sure enough, the beetle was turning around in the middle of the road. Car alarms blared as its metal body jolted several of the vehicles that were parked parallel to the sidewalk. Deep scratches were left in the frame.

"Why do I have a bad feeling about this one?" Push asked himself aloud.

"Um, I don't know," replied Scratch, giving him a funny look. "We took out those first two pretty easily."

"Yeah, I know," said Push, keeping both eyes focused on the approaching beetle. "It's just that, in all those comic books we've read, the last one is usually the hardest one to take down."

Wrath stepped through the small gap between them, nudging both men out of the way. Push started to get angry but then saw Wrath raise both hands above his head. As the beetle drew even closer, Wrath formed a ball of fire in the space between his two opened palms. Push and Scratch watched as the ball grew larger.

When it was as big as a house window, Push sank down to his knees and covered his head, in part only because of the heat. Scratch was following suit. By now, the fireball was floating above Wrath's head, several feet beyond his upraised hands.

The beetle never hesitated. Wrath stared the machine down with a stony expression, then launched the enormous fireball right at it. The ball of flame made contact, striking the metalsect in the face, exploding. The noise was intense, but the shock wave was even worse.

Push wasn't sure how he ended up tangled in the bushes. There was ringing in his ears, a terrible pain in his left arm, and twigs poking him through the fabric of his costume in several uncomfortable places. Furthermore, Scratch had somehow ended up on top of him. The weight wasn't helping his arm or the twigs poking him, but Push was too dazed for the moment to care one way or the other. The heaviness was actually comforting as he took stock of his injuries. Push tried to move his arm and found that he could. Though it was still sore, the initial pain wasn't hampering his ability to move it, meaning it most likely wasn't broken.

Still reeling from the blast, Push struggled to clear his head. Being so close to an explosion in real life was nothing at all like how it was portrayed in films. Push made a mental note of this as he struggled to focus his eyes on Scratch, who hadn't moved the whole time. Before his vision could clear enough, Scratch was already kissing him.

The gesture came out of nowhere, but Push wasn't about to complain. Though it was hardly the time or place, Push threw caution to the wind and wrapped both arms around Scratch's back to pull him in even closer. Scratch's coat felt slick, nowhere near as rough as it looked. His beard was tickling the hell out of Push's face as well. That thought gave Push pause.

Beard....

Push's eyes flew open and zeroed in on the face of the man above him. It wasn't Scratch who was kissing him.

Wrath held back slightly, far enough that Push was able to confirm that it was indeed him. Their lips barely touched, but as Push started to move away, Wrath pulled Push back into him. The kiss this time was rough, hard, and full of need. To Push's great shock, he was kissing back. The weight of Wrath's body pressed Push deeper into the ground and harder into the twigs. Push hoped the pain would snap him out of whatever sick joke his mind was playing on him, but it didn't.

Being so close together meant Push could feel the differences in their bodies now that he was more alert. The most obvious difference was in what lay between Wrath's legs. Push had no doubt that Wrath was very happy with where he was at the moment. The thing that startled him was just how large that happiness was.

Then again, he was having a hard time controlling himself as well.

Wrath suddenly jerked away, staring down at Push's face. His lips were swollen, and there were beads of sweat dotting his face. A cut marred the man's forehead, but otherwise, he didn't appear too worse for wear.

"We need to find Scratch," he said breathlessly.

Push could have died for forgetting about his boyfriend. "Get off me," he ordered in a near panic, struggling to shove Wrath away. "Get off now!"

But Wrath was already standing. Push ignored the hand Wrath extended to him and forced his way up onto his own two legs.

"Where's Scratch?" he demanded, thinking Wrath must have done something to him.

"I don't know," replied Wrath cautiously. "I woke up on top of you."

"Push!"

Push's heart leaped into his throat even as he felt the worst case of guilt crash into his gut. The sound of Scratch's voice made him look around frantically. Sighing, Wrath pointing directly behind where Push was facing, and when Push turned around, he felt a pair of familiar arms wrap around him.

"Thank God," Scratch said sincerely.

Scratch kissed him. Push could feel Wrath's eyes on them and didn't care in the slightest. Kissing his man back, Push savored the feel of his own arms being wrapped around his lover.

"I hate to be the one to interrupt," Wrath said a second later, "but we've got more problems."

Push moved away from Scratch, intent on reading Wrath the riot act. "Screaming," Scratch said, cutting Push off.

Wrath turned toward the noise, indicating to Push where it was coming from. "From the sound of things," Wrath continued, "our aliens have decided to come out of hiding."

Push felt the same sucker punch feeling to his gut, though for a different reason this time.

"This is it, then," Scratch said, reluctantly letting Push go.

Push knew what his boyfriend meant but couldn't bring himself to say it. Wrath had that covered, however.

"Time to go to war."

CHAPTER
SIX

THEY WERE everywhere.

"At least it's only a phalanx," Push overheard Wrath shout as one of the Clickers he'd been fighting exploded.

"What?" Scratch yelled back, fending off three of them with his cue stick. "Is this really a time for Marvel references?"

Push thrust his palm out and sent another Clicker flying, which swelled up and popped before it touched the ground. The goo spattered all over the ground and near Wrath's feet.

"There's always time for a quick Marvel reference," Push replied. "But what's that got to do with—"

"Not Marvel," Wrath corrected, sounding irritated as three Clickers went up in flames. "A phalanx is a group formation."

Even on fire, the Clickers expanded and popped like zits. "Scratch thought you were talking about techno-organic mutant-hunting robots," Push explained between gasps of air.

Wrath gave the two of them a look as Scratch joined them, having finished off his own group of alien zit bugs.

"Let's not give these bastards any ideas," Wrath suggested, looking a little alarmed now at the thought. "Things are bad enough as it is."

Push let out a long breath and nodded.

"It'd help if we could just get in touch with the others," Scratch grumbled. "We've been fighting these things since they marched down the street toward us. Where the fuck is everybody else?"

Push heard an angry clicking sound coming from behind them in the bushes. As he turned, a Clicker soldier armed with one of their laser arm blasters leaped out and took aim at his head. Before Push could fire off a telekinetic force bubble, a loud gunshot rang through the air. The Clicker jerked slightly while still in midmotion, like he'd been struck.

None of that stopped the creature's momentum, though. Push didn't have enough time to move out of the way. Both of them rolled backward into a tumble as the alien swelled up and exploded, coating him in a thick mucus.

"I hate when that happens," Push muttered, trying not to open his mouth too wide so the goo wouldn't go into his mouth.

"That answer your question, son?"

Sheriff Black's voice rang out clearly over the din coming from all around. "Took us a while to find your bunch. Care to fill me in on what you were doing all this time?"

Push stood up, slipping several times, and saw Black approaching them with several other officers, all of whom were armed with shotguns.

"I figured we'd run into you if we just kept looking for wherever there was trouble," Black said cheekily as he approached. "The rest of your bunch is on the other end of town, dealing with a fire that broke out when one of those bug critters blasted a propane tank."

Scratch looked impressed. "Um, you got all the way here from the other side of town that fast?" he marveled.

Black scowled. "We're not quite that efficient, fella," he said, holding up a walkie-talkie, "but these things sure do help."

Wrath looked as confused as Scratch was. "I thought the force field was cutting off all communications."

"Cell phones don't work," Black clarified. "Neither do land lines, because the force field cuts off anything that was being broadcast into the town from outside. Cell towers are located way outside city limits, and the phone company has to run lines through here."

"People are actually bitching that the cable isn't workin' either," an officer from farther back said, speaking up.

"Yeah," Black confirmed, rolling his eyes up toward a blacked-out street lamp hanging overhead. "The world's ending, but people still want the news."

"We just came from one of the side roads," Push said, taking the lead on his end and hoping no one paid too much attention to the alien slime coating him. "There were three metalsects working their way down the street."

Black frowned. "Funny thing about that," the sheriff said. "There were a couple of smaller ones near the local grocery. It looked kinda like they might've been snooping around for something."

"Where are they now?" Wrath asked, fire flashing in his palms momentarily.

"Ease off," Black said, holding a hand up. "We took care of them."

None of them said it, but Push could tell they were all thinking the same thing. Black could tell as well, and scowled.

"This ain't my first rodeo," he retorted in defense.

"He said they weren't that big," the same officer from before added, laughing quietly to himself.

"Shut your hole, Jones," Black barked, shaking his head.

"Any chance we could get some of those walkie-talkies?" Push asked, gesturing to the one Black had clipped back onto his belt. "With the phones down, none of us can communicate. It'd help if we all stayed on the same page."

Black chewed on that thought for a second. As his eyes widened, Push felt the hairs on his back tingle, and he turned toward the end of the street where the Clickers had come from. Wrath and Scratch mimicked the same movement. There, way on the other end, were more Clickers.

"This is our town," Black declared, cocking his shotgun. "We've got some of the local men volunteering to help us, but right now, I won't say no to anyone that wants to pitch in."

"Thanks," said Scratch, gripping his cue stick. "Nice to know we don't have to waste time fighting each other."

"Get to the police department," Black told them. "Tell them I sent you. They'll see about getting you and the others some equipment so we can keep touching base with each other."

Push turned back toward Black to thank the sheriff and saw he was fishing something out of his front pocket.

"Take my patrol car," Black said, tossing the keys to Push. "It's parked not far from here, around the corner, back the way we just came. You'll get where you're going faster if you take it."

"What about you guys?" Scratch asked.

The rest of the officers with Black each cocked their shotguns in answer. "We've got this," said Black confidently. "Get your spandex asses in gear."

The three of them broke into a run, moving side by side in the direction Black had indicated. Once they were far enough out of earshot, Push overheard Wrath mumble, "Okay, I'll admit it. That was pretty awesome."

The patrol car was parked crookedly on the side of the road halfway across a sidewalk. The hood was pointed toward someone's front yard. It looked like Black and his men had stopped and leaped out the minute they heard the fighting.

"Um," Scratch grunted. "He couldn't have parked closer?"

"Never mind," Push said, getting into the driver's seat. "Let's roll."

PUSH WASN'T sure why he'd expected the drive to the police station to go by fast or without incident. His mind was, in many ways at this point, operating on autopilot. As it happened, they arrived at the station a little over a half hour later even though it was not a long drive. It felt like every few feet they were stopping for something. People were out of their homes despite being told to remain inside, making themselves easy targets for Clickers.

Each time, one of them would jump out as soon as Push stopped the car to rectify the situation and herd the frantic pedestrians indoors. It was an easy enough process since the victims were being assaulted by stragglers of aliens and not whole platoons. The hard part was having to do it over and over again.

"You'd think people would learn," Wrath said when they stopped for the fourth time.

Silently, Push agreed with him but wasn't going to say so out loud. Now that the fighting had stopped for the moment, Push had a second to catch his breath and feel furious with Wrath for kissing him.

Never mind that Push had kissed him back even after realizing the truth. It hurt to admit it to himself, but Push knew he'd been in the wrong just as much as Wrath. The hard part was not being too angry at Wrath over it or blaming it all on him.

Push was slowly learning that he did not handle such responsibilities as well as he'd always assumed he did. The thought alone was bad enough, but now Push was having a personal conflict on top of the interplanetary one occurring right at that very moment. This was hardly the time for personal reflection or an identity crisis, so Push shoved his emotional baggage aside and floored the accelerator the moment Scratch was back inside the patrol car.

He would apologize to Scratch, beg for forgiveness if necessary, but later. Right now, there was a war of the worlds going on to deal with.

As it turned out, though, getting to the police station was the easy part. Even in the middle of a disaster on the scale they were facing, Push was in awe that there was no place to park. When the force field went up, several citizens of Shove Point evidently had gone to the cops to complain. There were cars parked all over the parking lot, many of them haphazardly, and more all over the road.

"Fuck this," Push declared, throwing the car in park as he slammed on the brakes.

The others leaped out along with him and trekked across the grass toward the building. Push zoomed in on the front doors using his goggles and switched to night vision mode. He'd turned the night vision on before climbing into the car. Without electricity, it was the only way he could see to fight. Power still worked in stored containers like vehicles and flashlights, but the city grid was offline.

Looking inside, Push saw what looked to be about a hundred people or more standing around in blankets and huddling together on the floor.

"It looks like the station has been turned into a safe house," he said, coming to a stop alongside one of the badly parked cars.

"Makes sense," replied Scratch, stopping next to him. "If this doesn't end soon, they'll need to find a bigger place to keep everyone."

Scratch's words made Push pause. He hadn't thought about tomorrow before. Everything had been so pandemic that there wasn't time. This could go on for days, weeks even, Push realized. They were looking at more than just a loss of power. Water could feasibly run out along with food. They were going to have to come up with some sort of system to keep track of everyone.

Push's head spun as the weight of this realization came crashing down. Standing up straight, he squared his shoulders as best he could and steeled his nerves.

"We'll think of something for everyone," Wrath said quietly, not looking anywhere near Push.

Push and Scratch looked at him, though, but before Wrath could say anything else, Scratch cut him off.

"We know," said Scratch in a somewhat humorous tone. "You're an empath. We remember. And we will."

Scratch gave Push a slap on the shoulder that turned into a very gentle, affectionate squeeze. "Count on it," Scratch said, his eyes trained solely on Push and nowhere else.

Push took the lead and marched up to the building doors. Several pairs of eyes turned to look as the three men marched inside. Push ignored them as best he could and swept the area for anyone wearing a uniform. There were kids huddled together under blankets, adults watching over them in droves, and people walking back and forth passing out battery-powered lanterns.

Push's eyes widened when he spotted an officer coming out of Black's office.

"Sir," he addressed, hoping his voice didn't sound tired.

The officer looked up and turned away slightly, as though about to duck back through the door he'd just come through.

"Sheriff Black sent us," Scratch said before the man could leave. "Um, he said you had walkie-talkies to spare."

The officer said nothing, looking back and forth from Scratch to Push and then finally behind them at Wrath.

"We can stand here and stare at each other," Wrath said, sounding irritated. "Or, we can get to work getting these people some help. And we'll do that a hell of a lot better if we can communicate."

Push scowled and was about to tell Wrath off, but the officer unexpectedly snapped out of his stupor and motioned for them to follow him.

"This way," the officer added in a strained voice. "We keep the extra supplies and equipment in a room down here."

Push followed along with Wrath and Scratch, stepping gingerly around the groups of people huddled together. Several of the younger members looked up and smiled at the sight of them. It occurred to Push that, as far as the kids were concerned, their fantasies had come true. Aliens had invaded, but the heroes were here to save them.

It made Push want to wet his tights. He could not have felt more ill-prepared for something like this. As one child flashed him a big grin, Push felt his stomach sink to new lows. They were all the hope these people had at the moment, which was enough to make him cry.

Nevertheless, he kept putting one foot in front of the other, marching forward with his head held as high as he could. The fun was officially over.

The three of them opted to wait outside in the narrow corridor while the officer fished the walkie-talkies out for them. A few minutes later, following some shuffling noises, the man emerged with one for each of them, as well as several spares.

"Thought you'd want a couple for your friends," he explained. "We don't keep extra batteries, but they oughta be fully charged."

"Thanks," Scratch replied, accepting his along with the extras.

"Now what?" Wrath asked as they worked their way back down the hall toward the main area.

"Um," Scratch said, slipping the spare walkie-talkies into his coat pockets, "we find the others and drop these off, then see what's going on around town. If we can commandeer another vehicle, it might be best to split up into teams of two."

Scratch turned sharply to look at Push. "Assuming that's okay with you," he added.

It took a second for Push to realize what Scratch was implying. When it finally hit him, the sinking feeling he'd been having in his stomach went all the way to his toes.

"We may not have to look far," Wrath said, interrupting. "Look who just came through the front doors."

They had just reached the main area. Push turned to where Wrath was indicating and saw Professor Trixter enter with Scarlet Queen, Marquita, and Rachel in tow.

"Thank God," Push said, exhaling.

Scarlet Queen spotted them first and motioned for the others to follow. "Here," Scratch said, digging each walkie-talkie back out again and passing them around. "Take these. The cops are using them to stay in touch with each other. They work under the force field, so we should be able to use them too."

"Kinda low tech," Rachel noted, accepting hers from Scratch.

"Better than nothing," said Marquita gravely. "We've been all over this stinkin' town trying to keep people in their homes and puttin' out fires."

"So we heard," said Push. "Nice job, by the way."

"Call me Dixie Whistler."

Push, Scratch, and Wrath all zeroed in on Marquita. Scarlet Queen snickered while Professor Trixter rolled his eyes toward the ceiling. Rachel remained stone faced.

"What?" Wrath asked, breaking the silence between them.

"They said we should pick code names or something," Marquita replied, like it should have been obvious. "Or whatever it is you call it. So I'm Dixie Whistler and she's Statique."

Marquita pointed to Rachel as she finished her sentence.

"Statique, huh?" Wrath asked, looking her over. "It fits, I guess."

"It's better than Greed," she admitted.

"Okay," Push said, going along with it. "Dixie Whistler and Statique, welcome to the Association. As an A-list ranking hero, I am hereby drafting both of you into the league with full credentials in light of the current crisis. You'll be formally inducted later, but for now, we have an invasion to stop and a city full of people to protect. Is that all right with both of you?"

"Fine by me, sugar water," Marquita, now christened as Dixie Whistler, said while giving one of her guns a twirl.

"Lead the way," Statique added.

They had barely taken two steps when Dixie Whistler looked back over her shoulder at Push and asked, "Do we get costumes? Because I really want a new costume. That old piece of shit Sloth used to have me wear was ridiculous."

Push couldn't help but laugh. "We'll figure something out for you both," he said, giving Rachel a look. "Assuming you both want them."

Rachel glanced at her girlfriend for a split second before letting out a tired sigh. "I might as well," she said. "Just don't stick me in anything black or gray, okay? It makes my butt look big."

"Don't look at me," Professor Trixter objected as they exited through the main doors one after the other. "I'm just a tech guy. Sewing is out of my league."

"Um, I can sew some," Scratch said, coming out last. "My grandmother taught me when I was little."

This earned Scratch a look of stunned surprise from Wrath.

"It helps if you know how to repair your own costumes after getting tossed around all night by punks jacked up on meth," Scratch retorted defensively.

"Makes sense to me," Wrath replied loftily. "Are you sure you're a straight guy, though?"

Push almost blasted Wrath into the police station for that remark, but Scratch just laughed along with Trixter and Scarlet Queen.

"Wait, he's straight?" Dixie Whistler asked, looking from Scratch to Push and back again in confusion. "I thought—"

"They are," Scarlet Queen answered before she could finish. "It's a little complicated."

In answer, Rachel took Dixie Whistler by her gloved hand. "Maybe not quite as complicated as you think," said Rachel, smiling.

"We need to move," Push said, though he hated interrupting. "There's still an invasion to stop. We don't know what the rest of the world looks like yet, so for right now, we focus on sorting out the mess all over town."

"Agreed, commander," Scarlet Queen said without a hint of sarcasm. "What are your orders, sir?"

Push looked from her to the rest of the group before settling on Professor Trixter. "Did you all come in the hovercraft?"

Trixter whipped his keys out from a coat pocket and held them up.

"Good," said Push. "Much as I hate taking you off the front line, we need to borrow your baby."

Without hesitation, Trixter tossed Push the keys. "She's insured," Trixter told him. "Just don't be too rough with her. I've seen how you drive."

"Yes, yes," Push grumbled, catching the keys and pocketing them while Wrath and Scratch both laughed.

"I'm going to drop you off at headquarters," he continued, motioning for everyone to follow as he marched out into the parking lot.

"That way," Scarlet Queen indicated quietly.

"Thanks," Push said, changing directions to where Trixter had parked the hovercraft far off to the side away from the haphazardly arranged cars. "I know you want to be out in the thick of this, Trixter, but we need you back at the house to help Wiccan Witch hold the fort and keep our gear up and running. You're sort of my key guy in all this."

"I can live with that," Trixter said cheekily.

"We need whatever you can cook up for us," Push resumed as they reached the hovercraft, which opened on command as Push hit the switch on the key ring.

Push went quiet as everyone climbed in. Wrath took the back seat next to Dixie Whistler and Statique. Scarlet Queen and Trixter sat in front of them while Scratch commandeered the passenger seat next to Push.

"Since there are eight of us," Push went on, starting the engine, "we'll divide up into teams of two. Trixter and Wiccan Witch are central command. Statique, since you and Dixie Whistler are used to working together, you'll take the upper side of town. Help where you can, but don't do anything to antagonize the locals unless they give you no other choice. We can't fight the alien invaders if we're too distracted fighting the citizenry."

"Understood," Statique said.

"Whatever you say, boss man," Dixie Whistler announced.

"Um, I'd like to go with Scarlet Queen, if you don't mind," Scratch said quietly as Push opened his mouth.

Push's jaw was left hanging open. "Why?" he asked, louder and faster than he meant to. "I mean, we can't have two super-powered people in the same group."

"Why not?" Scratch asked. "You and Wrath's powers complement each other. Look what happened when that metalsect exploded."

"Ha, I knew that word would catch on," Trixter said from in back.

Scratch ignored Trixter and resumed speaking. "I would've been dead if not for the two of you."

Push blinked. "What happened?" he wondered, thinking hard while trying to keep both eyes on the road. "I don't remember anything past the beetle machine exploding."

"You threw a telekinetic blast out at the same time Wrath threw fire at it," Scratch explained, looking surprised that Push didn't remember. "It took most of the edge off. The shockwave was the worst, but your blast took care of most of it. We'd be out of the game right now if not for both of you thinking so fast."

Push fell silent for a moment. "The countering shock wave must have been what knocked us apart," he muttered. "That's how I ended up in those bushes."

Push could feel his hands gripping the steering wheel the whole time. He was fighting the memory of what came after that along with the guilt of having inadvertently kissed Wrath. Now didn't feel like a great time to bring that up, but the more Push thought about it, the more he knew he was avoiding the real issue altogether.

"So I'll head out with Scarlet Queen," Scratch said. "We're familiar with each other, and that leaves you with Wrath to take out any metalsects left roaming around."

Push couldn't think of a good argument, so he kept quiet for the rest of the trip. There were fewer vehicles on the road at this point, so they made it to the house in good time.

"I'm off," Trixter said. "None of you had better end up alien lunch while I'm busting my ass making new gear for you all."

"Good luck," Push called out. "Keep Wiccan Witch safe."

"Wiccan Witch can take care of herself," Scarlet Queen said in defense of her friend.

"He knows," Scratch said quietly as Trixter shut the hovercraft door with a nod to Push. "Push meant something else."

Scarlet Queen started to turn toward Dixie Whistler and Statique but stopped herself in time.

"That's not suspicious," Dixie Whistler said, her voice carrying an edge. "Were any of you aware that we could hear you back here?"

"I think there's a theory in the Association that former villains are hard of hearing," Wrath said. "Though I haven't pinpointed where the idea began."

"We'll explain it to you later," Scarlet Queen said, looking directly at Push and not at Dixie Whistler or Wrath. "There's an invasion to stop."

"Long story short," Wrath cut in. "There's a space baby inside the house."

Push, Scratch, and Scarlet Queen turned around to shoot daggers toward Wrath. Statique and Dixie Whistler, meanwhile, were giving Wrath very bemused looks.

"Wait, you're serious?" asked Statique.

"We found a spacecraft right after we first got here," Wrath went on, ignoring the others. "It had this pod inside that was ejected when the craft blew up. Sloth was looking for it."

"Sloth?" Dixie Whistler frowned. "What does he want with a space brat?"

"No idea," Wrath answered, shrugging.

"Don't you think one of us should go ask him?" Statique asked, looking over at the others up front.

"Later," Push said, suddenly very tired and more annoyed than ever with Wrath. "Aliens and big metal bugs, remember? The timetable's pretty much full."

"Wiccan Witch is taking care of the kid," Wrath concluded. "It's kind of a secret right now, since we don't know what the aliens want with the kid or even if he belongs to them."

Statique looked less than impressed with Wrath's logic. "Is that really for any of us to decide?" she wondered, looking uncomfortable. "Aren't you putting people in danger?"

"They're aliens," Dixie Whistler insisted to Statique. "All the better reason to splatter them. Unless the kid is some kind of bug-eyed weirdo too?"

Dixie Whistler was speaking to Wrath now, who shook his head. "He's actually pretty cute," Wrath said, looking from Dixie to Statique. "He's just a kid, besides that."

Before Statique could respond, Wrath looked up at the front of the hovercraft. "So are we going now or not?" he asked Push.

"Depends," Scratch cut back scathingly. "You got any more secrets of ours you want to spill?"

"Push inducted them," Wrath replied calmly. "They're a part of the group now. Better we tell them what we're really fighting against instead of them finding out later on."

"He's right," Scarlet Queen said reluctantly, looking toward Push. "I'm still pissed, but he's right."

"So what are we doing?" Statique was speaking to everyone, but Push got the impression her question had been aimed at the woman sitting next to her.

"We're going," Push said as he pulled the hovercraft out into the street.

"Um," Scratch said hesitantly. "Actually, could we go back for just a second? I just remembered that I need to stock up on equipment."

Push slammed on the brakes and hit the switch to unlock the door. "Fuck," Push swore as Scratch took off for the house. "The fight will be over with by the time we get there!"

"Aliens across the universe, beware," he heard Wrath mutter.

"The heroes are on their way," Statique picked up. "Or they will be eventually."

CHAPTER
SEVEN

"ARE WE going to talk about it?"

Push felt his whole body go rigid. The others had already been dropped off at trouble spots, which left him alone with Wrath inside the hovercraft. The silence had been choking him, but Push preferred that to talking. Wrath was the last person he wanted to work with right now, or talk to for that matter.

"I wouldn't be here if Scratch hadn't insisted," Push stated flatly.

Wrath had been looking out the passenger window but turned when Push spoke. "I see," he said. "Were you afraid he would suspect something if you protested too much?"

Push gritted his teeth together. "You should know," he answered, feeling his jaw pop as he opened his mouth. "You're the one who keeps reminding everyone that you're an empath."

"You all keep forgetting."

Push's knuckles were turning white from him gripping the steering wheel. "Let's just drop it, okay?" he said with an undercurrent of pleading in his voice.

Wrath was quiet for maybe a total of three seconds. "Are you going to leave me to the bugs because I kissed you?" he then asked quietly.

Push almost slammed on the brake. "What?" he wondered, letting off the accelerator instead.

"I said," Wrath repeated, "are you—"

"Never mind," Push interjected. "I heard you the first time."

"You do that a lot," Wrath noted as the hovercraft coasted to a stop. "You ask me to repeat myself when you heard me the first time. Were you aware of that?"

"I just—" Push took a deep breath and hit the pedal again, causing the hovercraft to jump forward and making both their seats buck slightly.

"I'm not going to abandon you when we're in the thick of things," Push said finally. "I'm pissed at you—"

"You're mad at yourself," Wrath cut in. "You kissed me back because you thought I was Scratch. It was a simple mistake. Scratch isn't the type of man to hold that against you. I'm the one he's more likely to be mad at."

Push felt his anger abate a little as he thought Wrath's words over. "I'm taking the advice of an ex-con," he mumbled quietly, taking a turn much sharper than he should have. "I guess beggars can't be choosers."

"It's been a few days since you called me that," Wrath said, looking at Push while holding onto the door handle.

Push frowned. "Maybe I shouldn't have," he admitted, shifting in his seat as the hovercraft finally straightened out in the proper lane.

Wrath's eyes narrowed slightly as his mouth turned upward into a half smile. "I was a criminal," he said. "You were never wrong about that."

"No, but I shouldn't have rubbed it in your face," Push insisted. "You've done nothing but carry your weight and then some since… well, since we found you eating steak in our hotel room."

For some reason, Wrath laughed. "I considered running," he confessed, surprising Push. "At first, but only for a second. I felt like I had a second chance at life, even though I wasn't expecting anything good to come out of working for the Association. I knew they were using me, but it seemed like the lesser of evils."

"A deal with the devil you could live with?" Push offered.

"Something like that," Wrath said. "And then when Sloth entered the picture, I knew I was in this for the long haul."

Push smirked at that. "So how did it feel to watch your old boss go down and get carted off in chains?"

"Satisfying," Wrath replied, his voice dripping with smugness. "I bet Marquita and Rachel—"

"Dixie Whistler," Push corrected, "and Statique."

"Right," Wrath agreed. "I bet they feel the same way, though I won't be completely relaxed until I see Sloth, Envy, and Lust get carted off before a judge. If the Body Snatchers hadn't dropped in on us, I'd have insisted on following the cops to jail."

"I admire you having your priorities in order," Push commended. "Nice film reference, by the way."

Wrath's smile took on a bittersweet edge. "It was Pride's favorite film," he said softly. "We've been so busy beating down the havoc that I haven't even had the chance to ask Marq... Dixie Whistler and Statique about her."

"You're going to get the chance," Push assured him, bringing the hovercraft to a stop. "We just have to stay alive until then."

"Is that all?"

Push frowned as they reached a new sector of town. "Nothing here either," he muttered, getting nervous. "I'm beginning to worry."

"So am I," Wrath said. "Shouldn't there be more metalsects?"

"Don't complain," Push warned. "We may have gotten them all."

"I don't think we're that lucky," Wrath replied sourly. "But assuming you're right for just a moment, what do we do?"

"Go back and help wherever we can," Push answered simply. "There's still plenty to do, and we'll have other chances to kick some alien ass later on."

"Good," Wrath said, sounding satisfied. "So now that we've broken the ice and become best buds, do you want to know?"

"Know what?" Push asked without thinking.

"Why I kissed you."

Push slammed on the brakes, not because of Wrath's question but due to the road directly ahead of them catching fire. Wrath grabbed his door with one hand while casting the other outward at the windshield. The flames in front of the hovercraft bent away and extinguished as the craft slowed to a stop inches from them.

Sweat broke out over Wrath's forehead as he gritted his teeth. "Can't let the bag catch fire," he hissed, his voice strained with concentration.

"Trixter probably made the thing flame retardant," Push said, though his face creased with worry. "Still, this isn't a time to test that."

Wrath made a sweeping gesture with his free arm, and the flames in front of the hovercraft were swept away.

"What the hell happened?" he wondered. "It felt like the fire was trying to fight me off."

Push spotted movement overhead and leaned forward over the steering wheel. "That's what happened," he said gravely, pointing.

It was fast, but the metalsect flying above them slowed as it passed by their field of vision. Wrath's face went slack in surprise as what looked like a mechanical fly with helicopter rotors hovered above the road in front of them. Flames suddenly burst from twin barrels mounted on its front where the mouth might have been.

Wrath forced both hands forward and bent the flames away from the hovercraft, saving them both.

"If it keeps doing that," Wrath grumbled, "I'm going to get really irritated."

Push didn't reply. Throwing the hovercraft into reverse, he spun the wheel and raced backward away from the flames still pouring out of the metalsect. Spotting a parking lot, Push brought the craft around into a spin, sending the bag over a small border made of cement and several speed bumps. As the craft straightened out, Push saw they had rolled into the parking area of the local elementary school.

"Perfect," Wrath said, seeing where they were under the glare of the hovercraft's headlights. "Would it be a problem if we let that thing burn this whole place down first?"

"Come on," Push said, throwing his door open. "It's probably already on top of us, and I'd rather not die being burned alive inside this thing."

Wrath climbed out as well and met Push in back of the craft. "You won't die," Push overheard Wrath say quietly. "I will save you."

Push tried to tune Wrath out, but Wrath seized him by one arm. "I kissed you because I thought I'd never get the chance again," Wrath said, his voice sounding thicker than usual.

Push went tense. "This isn't really the time, Wrath," he insisted, feeling like a jerk nonetheless. "Did you see where it went?"

Wrath let go off Push's arm at once and looked away. "Sorry," Push said, kicking himself mentally. "I just—"

"I know," Wrath cut in, sounding hurt. "You're with Scratch. I should have known it would end up that way. Hell, if anything, it's my fault for pushing you two toward one another. I thought I'd get over it like I always had to."

The area was quiet save for the noise of the flames in the street not far away. Other than that, Push couldn't hear anything out of the ordinary.

"Did it leave?" he wondered out loud.

"Why would it just leave?" Wrath asked, though he no longer sounded upset.

Push turned automatically and gave Wrath his back. A second or two later, he felt Wrath close the gap between them. The two of them stood with their spines pressed together, searching the skies nearby.

"Why did it attack us?" Push asked himself and Wrath. "It set fire to the road and then flew off. Why?"

Wrath turned his head slightly toward Push. "Maybe that was it," he offered. "Maybe all it wanted was for us to get off the road."

"Why, though?" Push asked insistently. "This doesn't make any sense."

"It does." Wrath sounded certain now. "If it wanted us off the road and out of the vehicle, it makes a lot of sense, because now we're out in the open."

Neither of them moved.

"Things keep getting the drop on us," Wrath went on. Push could feel the man's body stiffening, and the sensation was having an effect on him. "I don't like it."

"So not the time," Push groaned, glancing down at himself.

"What?"

Push shook his head at Wrath's question and spotted something past a grove of trees farther back behind the main building.

"Nothing," he said. "Look over there. I think I've spotted our little firefly."

"Where?" Wrath whirled around, brushing his hand over Push's spandex-covered thigh in the process by accident.

"There!" Push pointed toward the trees, ignoring the tingling in his legs. "It's swooping back and forth past those trees."

Wrath frowned. "That's where the school gym used to be," he said. "Why would it be flying over there?"

"Let's go," said Push, already taking off.

"On foot?"

Push could hear Wrath's footsteps on the concrete catching up with him. "The hovercraft would be faster," Wrath breathed as he leveled his pace to fit Push's.

"And can be spotted faster," Push blurted out between breaths. "That's how the little bastard saw us in the first place."

The grove turned out to be slightly thicker than it looked in the dark. "Why in the world would anyone build a gym this far back from the school?" Push wondered out loud, wincing as a twig whipped across his face.

"The gym was built afterward," Wrath said, using his arm to block a second cluster of twigs from hitting Push. "Keep moving. Suddenly, I have a very bad feeling about this."

Thanks to Wrath's help, Push reached the clearing first. The firefly metalsect was zipping back and forth in circles around the roof of the gym.

"What could it want from this place?" he asked as Wrath stepped out of the trees.

"I sense something," Wrath said as the firefly paused to hover in front of the door. "It feels like there are people inside."

As Wrath finished speaking, the front door to the gym cracked open. A woman peeked out into the darkness and squinted at the two of them.

"Can I help you?" she asked, calling out hesitantly.

"Ma'am, get out of the building," Push called out, his attention alternating between her and the flying metalsect above. "It's not safe—"

Push never finished his sentence. The firefly swooped down, kicking up dust and dry grass with its rotors. Fire belched from the barrel mounts, covering the ground in front of the gym door. Push shoved Wrath back as the fire bent away from them under his command. Even with that, the heat was intense.

"That wasn't necessary," Wrath groaned, wincing slightly. "But thanks all the same."

"Never mind," Push said. "Bring that thing down before it torches the whole building."

Thrusting a palm out, Push fired a telekinetic blast straight for the firefly's left rotor, which clanged and rattled in response. Wrath raised both hands like he was fighting against the weight of something. The flames in front of the school bent upward and warped back toward the metalsect even as more poured down from it. Push could feel his eyes watering from the heat.

Wrath opened his mouth in a gasp and shouted one word. "Move!"

Small spouts made of fire exploded forth from the main body. Push had just sent another telekinetic blast at the firefly's underside and stopped short in awe. The flames struck the metalsect one after another, catching it off guard and sending it hurtling backward to safety.

"Awesome," Push admitted, before coming to his senses. "I mean, we still have to put the fire out, Wrath."

"It won't be easy," Wrath replied. He appeared to be trying to do that very thing. "That thing must be spraying napalm. This is a chemically created fire. It has fuel to burn on."

"So?"

The firefly swooped over again, shooting spurts of fire down at them. Wrath conjured several fireballs from the inferno in front of the gym and hurled each one up into the air as scatter fire to ward away the metalsect.

"Use your powers," Wrath shouted. "Blow out the flames with your telekinesis. That should do the trick. Just don't get any of the chemical on you or get too close."

"You think?" Push retorted back over the noise of the attacking mechanical nightmare and the fire in front of them.

Push stood facing the fire, bracing himself against the heat coming toward him. Gathering his inner strength, he forced both hands in front of himself, wincing as the temperature of the flames stung his palms. One after the other, Push launched telekinetic blasts into the fire, kicking clods of dirt into the air. Each time one of the force bubbles landed in the inferno, a portion of it fanned outward. It was enough to control the burning but not blow it out completely.

However, Wrath was doing his part by using the rising flames to fight the metalsect, which was still buzzing them every few seconds. It took all of Push's resolve not to duck and cover out of the way. Only the knowledge that the building was occupied kept his feet planted firmly on the ground.

The fire was more under control now, and Push was keeping it from getting any closer to the gym. Feeling angry, frustrated, and overheated from being too close to the flames, Push jumped back when the firefly zipped above his head yet again.

Pouring all of his negative emotions into his hands, Push concentrated the energy he felt there into a telekinetic bomb, a very potent one.

"Hold it still," he called out to Wrath, not bothering to look up. "I'm going to try something."

"I can't," Wrath shouted back. "It's too fast. I'm doing all I can trying to hit this thing."

"Then burn this instead!"

Push raised both arms high so Wrath could see. As he looked up, the metalsect paused in midair, several feet higher than before. Push took aim and zeroed in on the firefly with his goggles, then tossed the telekinetic bomb one-handed. Wrath saw what Push was doing and gathered the fire burning across the ground in front of the gym. A glowing ball of fire and light rose off the ground and flew straight up into the air.

Both balls fused together, merging into one before they struck the underside of the metalsect. The firefly didn't even bother trying to move. The attack tore open its belly, setting the whole interior ablaze. Wrath backed up several steps, then turned and ran, grabbing Push by the arm in the process. Fortunately, there was no reason for him to get excited. The damaged firefly swerved into a downward arc thanks to the one remaining functioning rotor.

Wrath and Push stopped and turned around just in time to watch the metalsect crash into the main elementary school building and explode on impact.

"That should make some kids happy," Wrath said with a satisfied look on his face. "Assuming school wasn't canceled already due to alien invaders."

Push laughed and noticed Wrath hadn't let go of his arm. Wrath saw this and immediately let go, taking several steps sideways for good measure.

"Sorry," he muttered. "I forgot myself."

Push opened his mouth but found he had nothing to offer Wrath. "You were trying to save me," he tried instead, fumbling with his words like a fourteen-year-old. "I appreciate it."

"You did the same," Wrath pointed out, refusing to make eye contact.

"I know," replied Push, feeling out of his element somehow. "It's what we do. Scratch and I… and Wiccan Witch, Scarlet Queen, Trixter…. We watch each other's backs. That's just how we do it when we're together. None of us think much about it anymore."

Wrath stepped forward then. Push watched him approach the remaining flames still burning intensely in front of the gym. It occurred to him that he should follow, that Wrath could probably use a hand, but his feet wouldn't move. Instead, he watched as Wrath stopped a few feet from the fire. The heat didn't appear to affect him. Wrath raised both of his arms high overhead and brought them down. The fire buckled and bent as though an enormous fan had blown over it. Wrath repeated the gesture, occasionally raising his arms instead to bring the flames up higher before blowing them down again.

Soon, he had the fire more or less out, save for a few patches here and there. Telling himself it was safe now and that there was no other reason for him to be keeping his distance, Push made himself walk over to Wrath's side.

"It's easier to do this when there are no distractions," Wrath said, once Push was within earshot. "Just in case you thought I was screwing around before."

Push frowned and gave Wrath a startled glare. "It never entered my mind," he said, a little more defensively than he'd intended.

"Oh," Wrath replied, looking away. "Sorry. My mistake."

The door to the gym opened, giving Push a reprieve from having to speak again. A woman with curly hair was looking timidly out into the darkness. Push wasn't completely sure, but it looked like the same one from earlier.

"Sorry for the disturbance," Wrath told her. "How many people are in there?"

The woman straightened up and adjusted her shirt. "Three dozen or so," she answered, sounding more confident than Push had been expecting. "We were holding a prayer service."

Push thought he saw a wry smirk appear on Wrath's face for a brief second before it went flat.

"It may not be safe here, ma'am," Push warned, stepping up. "The sheriff has issued orders for people to stay in their homes."

"We're no safer in our homes," she replied. "It's the end of the world."

That made Push hesitate.

"The end of the world," Wrath said flatly. "Naturally. Revelations specifically mentioned bug-faced aliens and force fields surrounding out-of-the-way towns."

"Not now," Push chided, though nowhere as harsh as he'd intended to sound. "Ma'am," he tried again, calling to the woman in the doorway.

Something made Push pause. He could hear things coming toward them, and they sounded familiar. Wrath looked up at the same time Push did.

"Get out of there!" Push screamed, looking back at the woman. "Now!"

Push started to move, but it was already too late. High overhead, three metalsects plunged toward them out of the sky. There wasn't time to see how they'd arrived. Push had heard rotor noises and what might have been the sound of multiple engines as well. None of that mattered, though. Push tried to run toward the gym, to at least save the woman despite knowing there wasn't time, but Wrath dragged him away.

"Let me go!" he heard himself shout.

Push wasn't sure what he could do, didn't know if there was anything to do. It all happened so fast. Things felt like they were fast-forwarding while his and Wrath's bodies moved in slow motion. Wrath yanked on Push hard suddenly, folding both arms around his chest and pulling Push into him as they rolled to the side.

Debris was already flying. Three metalsects, a spider, a mantis, and a scorpion, had fallen on top of the gym. It amazed Push that his brain had been able to absorb that much given how fast it all went. The combined size and mass of the three machines was enough to bring the roof of the gym crashing down. There was an unearthly sound of metal tearing and plywood snapping to pieces.

Push and Wrath were rolling along the ground. Dust and debris flew everywhere over their heads. Push was still fighting Wrath's grip, but the pyrokinetic wouldn't let him go. There were no screams to fill the air. Push thought someone should have cried out, but it had all happened too fast.

They were all dead. Every last man, woman, and possibly child were either lying dead under the rubble or being crushed by the metalsects' feet.

Push gasped for air and found he wasn't being held too tightly to breathe. "Let me go," he ordered Wrath, who still hadn't released him.

Wrath wouldn't budge.

"Let me go, Wrath," he screamed. "Those people... they're trapped in... they need our help, Wrath!"

"They're dead," Wrath answered.

Push tried to shove Wrath away from him, and Wrath obediently complied by letting Push go. "They're not dead," Push insisted, struggling to get to his feet. "They can't be...."

Wrath stood up smoothly, like it was no effort for him at all. "They're dead," he repeated. "I can feel them."

"We're standing right here," Push snarled. "We were... right there, Wrath."

"I know," Wrath said quietly, somehow making himself heard over the metalsects, which were crawling out of the gym debris toward them now. "And so are they, Push."

Push turned, not registering the machines struggling to free themselves. All he saw was the wreckage of the gym beneath their numerous legs. He could hear the metal limbs crunch as they stomped out of the shambles.

Finally, his eyes focused.

"What do we do?" he heard someone ask.

Thinking it was Wrath, Push turned toward the pyrokinetic, who was staring down with a look of surprise on his face. It hit Push that he'd been the one to ask.

"We fight," Wrath answered. "Or we run. There aren't any other answers for the moment that I can see."

Push and Wrath started inching backward. "I've never run before," he admitted. "Not really. I've lured muggers into a false sense of security, but I never full-on retreated."

"First time for everything," said Wrath.

The metalsects were completely out of the gym rubble now and heading toward them with a purpose.

"We took three of these things before," Push pointed out hopefully.

"There were three of us," Wrath replied, cutting him down. "And somehow, these feel like they're cut from a tougher mold than the last."

Push swallowed, took one more look at the spider metalsect, which was watching him in particular with all eight of its shiny red-lighted eyes, and turned.

"Run!" he shouted.

Wrath needed no further convincing. "Let discretion be the better part of valor," he called out, following fast on Push's heels.

CHAPTER
EIGHT

WRATH MADE it to the hovercraft ahead of Push.

"Keys!" Wrath shouted.

Push fished them out and tossed them into Wrath's hands as he ran to the other side of the hovercraft. The metalsects were ripping their way through the barrier of trees. That had been enough to slow them down momentarily but not stop them, though Push wasn't surprised. The most they could hope for was the metalsects losing ground long enough for them to escape.

Push didn't even care that he'd given the wheel to Wrath. Jumping inside, he slammed the door shut and buckled himself in as Wrath slipped the keys into the ignition and slammed a thumb down on the starter.

The hovercraft roared to life. Wrath reached for the controls, flung the gear into drive, and tore off across the parking barrier before the bag underneath the craft had fully inflated. The metal scraped against the concrete, but Wrath kept going.

"Who gave you driving lessons?" Push wondered.

"I've been taking notes," Wrath answered, as if it were obvious. "I learned how to drive before I had mastered my powers. Sloth sometimes had me work as the wheel man on jobs where muscle wasn't a requirement. Something about me pulling my weight."

"But you haven't driven in years." Push wasn't sure why he couldn't let the subject die, though a quiet voice in his head whispered that he was just trying to get away from what had happened. "How can you—"

"Not now!"

Wrath turned the wheel sharply, whipping the hovercraft too hard and sending it gliding through the front yard of a nearby house. Push held on for dear life as Wrath corrected himself, pulling the craft around into a new turn that brought them back onto the street.

"They'll never miss those lawn gnomes," Push overheard Wrath mutter.

"I want Scratch to ride with you," Push declared as he struggled to straighten himself back up in the seat. "He'll never complain about the way I drive again."

Looking in the rearview mirror, Push saw the metalsects moving in on their tail. "It would be this much worse," he growled.

"Check the controls," Wrath ordered, gripping the wheel tightly as he swerved the hovercraft back and forth in an effort to lose the metalsects.

"What?" Push wondered, looking at the glowing dashboard. "What for?"

"Weapons," Wrath replied. "Explosives. Leftover missiles. Laser cannons. Anything on this crate that we can use to take those machines out before they catch up to us and tear this thing to pieces with us inside."

Push argued no further. Professor Trixter had already used up the hovercraft's defense weapons during their fight with the Trash Titans. However, given the current situation, Push was not willing to overlook the possibility that Trixter might have been wrong.

That, and the alternative was sitting quietly while giant robot insects ate them alive.

"Nothing," Push muttered, rolling through several different screen windows. "Those are all used up. Wait, this might be something."

Hot air rushed from the vents, hitting Push directly across the face. "Sorry," he said loudly as Wrath spun the wheel again and twisted the hovercraft into a sharp turn that left them facing backward.

"That was the heater," he said, shutting the air off as Wrath slammed the craft into reverse and kept going backward.

Static blared out from the speakers as Wrath spun them sideways so that the craft was driving forward again.

"That was the radio," Push muttered, pushing a button to turn it off, but instead it switched stations to more static.

"I noticed," Wrath said. "Keep trying. I'll see what I can do about losing them."

Wrath hit the accelerator as Push killed the radio. "You can't let them chase us all over town," Push protested. "They'll tear it to pieces trying to get us."

"We run or we get out and fight," Wrath hissed through gritted teeth. "I'm actually not happy about it either, much as I hate to admit it."

Push looked over his seat through the rear window. The scorpion metalsect was currently in the lead. The mantis was having a harder time keeping up, but the spider looked to be right on the scorpion's metal stinger.

"I always wanted something to tear this whole burb apart," Wrath went on, "but not while I was trapped in it."

"The scorpion's gaining on us," Push warned.

The hovercraft rattled as the scorpion's metal footfalls shook the ground underneath them. Push looked again and wished he hadn't.

"Not for long," said Wrath, keeping both eyes on the road. "I have an idea."

Push held on for dear life once again as Wrath's foot hit the floor. The craft bucked forward, putting them just out of reach of the metalsect scorpion as it swung a claw at their rear bumper. The hovercraft surged over the crest of a steep hill, leaving the ground and their pursuers behind briefly. Both men grunted when the craft came back down.

"Where are we going?" Push wondered as Wrath turned the hovercraft onto a set of train tracks that ran through town.

"To the border," Wrath said.

The cabin inside the hovercraft was filled with a dull, steady noise as the air bag underneath them raced over the two metal rails. Behind them, however, there was a much bigger cavalcade of sound. The metalsects, caught off guard by Wrath's driving, had crashed into one another. The result was a pile of tangled legs and angry-sounding chirping.

Wrath slowed the hovercraft down as the mantis got up first, leaving the spider and the scorpion behind.

"We don't want to lose them too soon," Wrath said. "Not while they're still in town."

"Care to fill me in on this plan of yours?" Push asked, looking behind past the mantis at the other two machines, both of whom were righting themselves now and in hot pursuit as well.

Wrath saw the same thing Push did and applied pressure to the accelerator once again. "I'm testing a theory," he continued, "and hopefully getting rid of these three B-grade sci-fi-flick rejects as well."

Facing forward again, Push reached for the dashboard and resumed looking for auxiliary weapons.

"Sounds great," he said, turning the windshield wipers on by accident. "How do you plan on doing all that, though?"

It sounded like they were discussing the weather instead of fleeing from abominations of technology.

"The force field," Wrath said as the wipers went back down and the air-conditioning came on instead. "I've thought about something. Just how difficult would it be for something to bust through it if enough pressure were applied?"

"Dunno," Push admitted, as the seat beneath him began humming. "Dammit, Trixter. What sort of emergency requires the passengers to get a full-shiatsu massage?"

"I want to try that later," Wrath interjected, speeding up as the metalsects caught up to one another. "Anyway, if we can lure these three to the border where that force field is, we may be able to kill two birds with one stone."

"I like it," Push said, giving up on the controls. "Makes me wish I'd thought of it sooner. We should have been trying to get people out of here before now."

Wrath caught the tone in Push's voice and looked across at him. "Don't start beating yourself up over it right now," he said insistently. "We need you to think clearly, and our first priority was keeping the town from tearing itself apart."

"Still," Push grumbled, more at himself than Wrath. "It was stupid."

"Giant monsters are chasing us," Wrath reminded, pushing the hovercraft to its limits. "Is this really a good time for you to be having an existential crisis?"

Push looked back yet again, to find all three mechanical monsters were closing in once more. Desperate, his eyes swept back over the dashboard, hoping to find something that would deter the metalsects for at least a few moments.

"Where the hell is that barrier?" Wrath shouted all of a sudden, startling Push enough that his elbow struck the dash.

The lighted dashboard abruptly went black. "Fuck!" Push swore. "What did I do?"

A small panel suddenly brightened in the middle, above where the stereo and air conditioning controls had been.

"It cannot have been that easy," Push whispered, reaching out to touch the glowing square panel in the center.

"Do you know what you're doing?" Wrath asked, sounding uncharacteristically nervous all of a sudden.

"I haven't got a clue," Push retorted. "Let's hope this does something good."

Push pressed his palm to the glowing panel. The square changed from blue to red in a flash. Push didn't have time to worry that he'd done the wrong thing again. A noise like a "klunk" sounded somewhere in back, followed by two quick whirls. Without warning, the hovercraft was thrown up into the air off the train tracks.

"The hell did you just do?" Wrath screamed, gripping the steering wheel for dear life.

The craft came crashing back down to the side off the tracks before Push could answer, not that he would have known what to say. The engines roared as the craft bucked, straining to move. Whatever was holding it in place, however, wouldn't let go. Push looked out the rear window and saw twin cables extending out of the rear of the craft. The thick cables had latched on to the spider metalsect and imbedded themselves in its face.

Meanwhile, the other two metalsects were moving around it, trying to get to the hovercraft, which was locked firmly in place. Desperately, Push scanned the dashboard again for what he hoped would be a release. Spotting the square panel again, he noticed it was flashing back and forth between red and green.

"Let's hope this does it," he whispered, slamming his fist down.

The panel glowed green, but the cables remained caught on the spider. Instead of releasing, sparks flew out of the caught metalsect's face. On either side, the mantis and scorpion were closing in.

"Fuck's sake, let go already!"

Push's fist hit the panel yet again as he cussed. Both cables snapped free of the spider metalsect and retracted back into the rear compartment of the hovercraft. Wrath, meanwhile, hadn't let his foot up off the accelerator the whole time. The moment the cables let go, the craft bucked forward hard and took off over the grass.

"Maybe you shouldn't touch any more buttons," Wrath said tensely, keeping both hands firmly on the wheel.

"Good idea," Push agreed.

The metalsects were still in pursuit of them. The brief stop they'd made, however, meant the craft had taken a steady lead. The glow of the barrier was bathing the trees they raced past with a bright-green color, making them stand out. It also made seeing in the darkness much easier.

"We're getting close," Wrath said. "It's like the air in this part of the woods is supercharged with something."

"Ionization," Push said. "Like when lightning is about to strike."

"Maybe we could use that to our advantage." Wrath hit the brakes as he finished speaking. "No better time than now to find out."

"What are you doing?" Push demanded, seizing the handle on his door as Wrath popped his own.

"Getting out," Wrath replied. "Look straight ahead."

Push did and reached for the controls on his goggles automatically. "There's too much interference here," he said as his goggles went white with static. "I can't see anything while my goggles are turned on."

"So I wonder how those three will handle it," said Wrath, before hopping out onto the ground.

Push swore under his breath and threw open his door, muttering, "He's worse than Scratch is," as his feet hit the grass.

The metalsects were in the distance, coming down the track fast toward them. "What's this plan?" Push asked, feeling his knees weaken. "It'd better be a good one, because if we die here—"

The mantis let out a shriek, the familiar sound of electric crickets and metal shredding, only this one was at a much higher pitch.

"Never mind," Push muttered after he'd uncovered his ears.

"We're going to lure them toward the force field," Wrath explained before swallowing hard. "I foresee one of two things happening. The field will either come down because of the metalsects slamming into it, or the force field will fry their circuits."

The closer the metalsects got, the slower their movements were. This didn't escape Push's notice.

"It doesn't look as though they like it here," Push said. "The ionization is worse this close to the barrier."

"We need every advantage we can."

Push considered Wrath's statement as the metalsects picked up speed again, their movements more jerky and robotic than earlier during the chase.

"Wait," Push said. "Are you going to stand there and tell me that your big plan consisted of us both standing here and hoping those three things tripped over one another trying to get to us, and rolling into a big cartoon ball right at the force field?"

Wrath frowned. "I wasn't thinking exactly in those terms," he replied, sounding put out by Push's lack of faith. "I'm pretty sure all three won't stick together into one big ball long enough for them to roll very far."

Push glowered at Wrath.

"You will note," Wrath began, moving back suddenly, "that I never said it was a very good plan."

Push looked up at the metalsects bearing down on him now and flung his hand out, striking the spider in the face once before running backward after Wrath.

"I'm going to kill him," he muttered, staring at Wrath's retreating back. "I'm going to kill him for this once it's all over."

The spider charged, its metallic pincers snapping angrily as the distance between it and Push lessened. Push shot another telekinetic blast at the beast, which kept it from closing those last few inches. The other metalsects were racing right alongside the spider. Push saw Wrath send several fireballs through the air at them and sighed inwardly with relief.

Push thought he could see the barrier just up ahead. This close, his goggles were shorting out on him, so Push spared a step to nudge them off the bridge of his nose into his bangs. Up ahead, Wrath stood before the force field, keeping the metalsects off Push's heels with what might have been flaming spears. Sparks flew now, landing on the grass surrounding the metal tracks. Push guessed the metalsects were beginning to short out. Whatever was going wrong behind him, it wasn't enough to slow any of the three mechanical nightmares down.

The part of the track where the force field intersected was sliced clean through. It looked like the barrier had cut through the iron like a hot knife through butter. The thought made Push's stomach clench for a second, but there wasn't time to dwell on it further.

Wrath had both arms out and grabbed Push as he tried to run past. Both rolled off to the side, the air around them crackling. Push could feel his hair standing on end now. The air around them was popping. It reminded Push of a box of bullets he'd seen explode in a fireplace on television once.

"I don't think they're coming any closer," Push said, getting up.

"The charged air in this section of the woods must be shorting out the nanobots holding the metalsects together," Wrath reasoned, before adding sharply, "And please don't correct me by saying 'microbots.'"

"I wasn't going to," Push said. "I'm too busy weighing the likelihood of us living through the ordeal."

"We'll never get a better chance if we don't do it now," said Wrath, glancing at Push. "Can you pull off another telekinetic bomb?"

"I don't know," Push answered truthfully. "These things are pretty big, and I won't be much good to you afterward."

Wrath thought for a second. "Work your way around them," he said, before easing away from Push. "Get behind and try to herd them farther down into the barrier."

"On three?" Push suggested, doing the same as Wrath now but in the opposite direction.

"Sounds good," Wrath agreed. "Three!"

Push bolted, keeping his eyes on the space ahead of him, counting out each footfall as it thudded against the solid ground beneath his feet. He wasn't looking off to the side where he knew Wrath would be. There was no time, and it would slow him down. Losing speed was not an option for him at this point. The metalsects had started to turn the moment he took off. Push kept glancing up at them, especially the towering mantis.

Even this was distracting, but he had to know where his enemies were. It was a simple combat principle, though he doubted anyone at the Association training camp had been thinking of this particular situation when they were instructing him and Scratch.

It almost made him laugh out loud.

The uneven ground made running difficult. Since he couldn't use the night vision on his goggles, Push was having trouble keeping an even pace. Still, he made it around the metalsects, who were thankfully much slower than the giant robots on cartoon shows and old Power Rangers reruns.

"Now," he heard Wrath call out.

There was a bright flash of red, signifying Wrath's location. Push gathered up every last bit of strength he had in him, then dug deeper. The bursts of flames from Wrath and his own telekinetic force bubbles struck against the metal hides of the monsters. Push spotted Wrath working his way in a semicircle toward him and did the same.

"Our powers work better when combined," Wrath said. "Let's team up."

The metalsects weren't doing well in the ionized atmosphere. Their movements were even jerkier and more robotic than before. Wrath summoned flames to his hands, shaping them into spheres. When Push flung a telekinetic blast, Wrath would release the sphere at the same time. The two combined in midair, exploding like a stick of dynamite in the mantis's face.

"Again!" Push shouted.

Their second attack sent the spider reeling. The scorpion had looked ready to charge but stepped back tentatively all of a sudden, as though reconsidering.

"Aim for the mantis again," Wrath suggested. "We'll take them on one at a time while they're disoriented."

"Good call," Push acknowledged.

Their next combined blast struck the mantis on its long neck. The creature abruptly swung itself around in a very awkward turn that looked like it almost caused the metal beast to topple from the momentum.

"Keep it up," Push ordered. "I think it's working!"

As their following attack blew away the metal scorpion robot's stinger halfway down the appendage, the whole area was lit up like a Fourth of July celebration all at once. Farther back behind the scorpion and spider, Push could see the mantis twitching uncontrollably. The air around them crackled, causing what little hair Push had that wasn't standing up to stick out in all directions.

Looking down, he saw with great relief that neither he nor Wrath was standing on the metal rails.

"Don't stop," Push ordered.

Neither remaining metalsect had turned back or made a move to help their ally. Push kept up his telekinetic assault, aided by Wrath's pyrokinesis, driving both machines in the direction of the barrier. The force field was now clearly outlined. The mantis hadn't budged. The sight reminded Push of a great big wasp he'd once seen get too close to a bug zapper. The machine couldn't draw away from the field.

The scorpion struck the field next with what remained of its tail. The instant the tip touched the barrier, the entire metal body went spastic. Instead of moving away from the barrier, however, the machine was lifted off the ground toward it. Push stared in awe and shock as the metal scorpion beast was pressed against the force field like a bug caught in a spider's web.

"I wasn't expecting that," Wrath said, sounding eerily calm.

"I think the force field has electromagnetized the metalsects caught inside of it," Push reasoned, before what he'd just said registered. "I spend way too much time on the phone with Trixter."

"Does that mean we're next?" Wrath wondered, looking at Push worriedly now.

The spider, the last remaining metalsect, wasn't looking so well. Its legs clawed at the ground like it was being dragged backward. A moment later, it was hanging in the air between the scorpion's legs and what little remained of the mantis's head.

"Maybe we should run again," Push said, backing up.

"I agree," concurred Wrath.

As they broke into a run together, Push remembered the hovercraft and looked back. The craft was gliding across the ground on the airbag, heading on a collision course for the spot where the metalsects hung. Push winced and shielded his face as the craft hit.

The explosion that followed was unexpected, though by this point, Push was getting used to things blowing up near him. This time, he turned toward the blast and threw out a telekinetic burst as wide as possible to flank both him and Wrath. The force struck the bubble, pushing it back toward them, but Push didn't relent. The air sizzled as the ambient ions were sucked into his telekinetic field. Push had no clue how the science worked, but he was open to any available help.

When the shock wave abated, both men were left standing on their own two feet. Push didn't keep that status for very long, however, sinking to his knees as his strength finally gave out.

"Thanks," Wrath said, getting down on one knee beside him.

"Sure," Push gasped. "Just let me catch my breath."

The ground near the force barrier was singed. There was metal shrapnel and rubble much farther out, however. Much of it was what remained of the three metalsects, though Push recognized pieces of the hovercraft mixed in as well.

"Trixter will kill me for this," Push croaked softly, more from exhaustion than worry.

Slowly, the two of them got to their feet. Push used Wrath's shoulder to steady himself, something he regretted doing at once. The moment his hand touched Wrath, Push felt a jolt race through his bloodstream. There were several layers of fabric separating their skin, but that couldn't stop whatever Push was feeling.

Wrath wasn't gentle. He didn't take Push gently into his arms. Push didn't wait to be held like something off a poster in an old black-and-white film. They were clawing at one another in seconds, scratching and grasping at each other's clothes, rooting around for an access point.

It didn't feel the way Push was expecting it to. His mind had shut off. He wasn't screaming and cursing himself for what he was doing. Push was well aware of what he was doing too. With a frustrated growl that startled him, his hand managed to work its way up inside Wrath's black shirt and feel the warm skin holding in very tight muscles. Upward, his hand roamed until it reached Wrath's left nipple.

The moment his fingers brushed the taut nub there, Wrath moaned.

"What are we doing?" Push asked out loud.

"This," Wrath said as he cupped Push's rock-hard cock, straining in his spandex pants. Feeling the man's hand there, just as warm and urgent as his, made Push realize how uncomfortable he was.

Wrath sensed this and bent down to scoop Push up in his arms. The gesture threw Push for a loop. He hadn't pictured Wrath as weak, exactly. The man was taller, certainly, and well developed, but Push made up for his diminutive stature by being packed with extra strength. He'd never relied on his telekinesis until recently. Wrath, evidently, didn't depend on his flame powers too much either, for he was able to carry Push off to the side with ease.

Several seconds passed before it occurred to Push that he should feel bothered by being carted around. Bigger guys had always treated him like he was lesser for being small. This didn't feel like the same thing, though. Wrath had been lovingly kissing his neck the whole time.

Push looked around to see where they were going and spotted what looked like a singed sofa cushion a little farther down. Wrath was making a straight line for it as he shifted his balance to keep Push aloft in his arms. As they drew closer, Push realized the cushion was actually one of the chairs from the hovercraft. The explosion had blasted it quite a ways from the barrier.

As Wrath stopped in front of the hovercraft seat, he lowered Push down onto it, kissing him the whole time. Push kissed back, surprised by his own eagerness, and fumbled with the front of Wrath's pants. Wrath shrugged out of his long coat and yanked the dark rocker's T-shirt over his head, revealing the pale, fuzz-covered skin to the night air. Push had the man's cock in his mouth. The shaft was hard, long, and almost as thick as a beer can. He could remember seeing Wrath giving Scratch head a couple of nights after their arrival in Shove Point. His memory of that moment was somewhat faded. Much as he tried, he couldn't remember giving Wrath much attention. Push's eyes had been for Scratch and no one else.

Now Push was licking the shaft from tip to root, covering it in his spit. Wrath, meanwhile, had shucked his pants and was gingerly stepping out of them, careful not to stray too far from Push's eager hands and face.

When Wrath reached behind Push, Push expected the taller man to force him down onto his cock. Instead, Wrath seized a handful of fabric in his fist and yanked hard. Realizing what the man wanted, Push reached around with one arm and helped tug the upper half of his uniform over his head. This meant taking his mouth off Wrath's dick momentarily, but Wrath was all too happy to help guide Push back onto it once Push was as bare-chested as him.

Next came Push's spandex pants. Push helped himself out of those along with his jock strap. The cup fell to the side in a mixed pile of their clothes. Now that they were both naked, Push felt himself being urged away from Wrath's dick.

Push tried to resist, but Wrath was adamant. When Push looked up curiously, Wrath was staring down at him. The dark-haired man's mouth was open. A light breeze sent several sweat-coated locks across his face. Wrath looked to be trying to form words, but he failed. Push continued to stare as Wrath gazed down as though he were trying to drink Push into him through his eyes.

Push blinked, and Wrath was in his face. Before Push could flinch, Wrath was kissing him, urging him backward to lie down on the seat. Push tried to fight at first, but his body wouldn't cooperate. When Wrath was stretched out on top of him, the weight of his tight body pressing Push deeper into the seat, Wrath began kissing his way down

Push's chest. At each nipple, Wrath paused to lick and tease. The sensations made Push moan, begging wordlessly for more.

Push felt out of control in a way he couldn't describe, partly because he couldn't think straight. He was aggressive in bed. Push was always a dominant lover, especially with guys bigger than him. One had suggested years ago that he preferred to top as some sort of compensation for his size and height. The guy had been a psychology student, and their relationship hadn't lasted long. It had been food for thought, though, and something Push occasionally wondered about.

Wrath was totally in control, but more surprising was how eager Push's body was to give that control over to Wrath. The pyrokinetic was currently licking at the crevices of his abs. Sweat had gathered there in copious amounts, and from the way Wrath lapped away at it, Push could assume he was a man on a mission to drink every last drop.

Wrath rose, looking Push dead in the eyes. Push watched as Wrath dragged his body closer using both hands on Push's hips. A shock of fear went through Push, but he relaxed as Wrath began turning himself around so that his head was pointed toward Push's cock. Wrath's own manhood floated above Push's face for a moment before the pyrokinetic lowered himself all the way down.

Push gasped as he felt Wrath's mouth on his dick and opened his jaw wider to allow for the unsettling girth the firebug possessed.

A gurgling noise escaped through Push's mouth as the tip hit the back of his throat. Wrath, meanwhile, was sucking down Push's shaft like he was possessed by a cum-guzzling ghost, eager to take the juice from Push's balls. Push forced himself to take more of Wrath's own thick meat, breathing in and out furiously through his nose as he felt the cudgel stretch his throat. It hurt, but the pain was making Push motivated. Wrath had all but inhaled Push's dick, and Push wasn't about to let himself be outdone.

While Push used his tongue to lap at the foreskin covering the head of Wrath's dick, his hands eagerly explored the pyrokinetic's body. Wrath's skin burned hot like scalding water. It felt like Push was being given fellatio by a humanoid furnace. It should have stung, but the sensation left pricks all across his torso and abdomen. The feeling left Push wanting more, so much that when Wrath parted his legs and reached down farther to lap at Push's hole, Push let him without a word of protest.

Feeling that turnabout was fair play, Push removed Wrath's cock from his throat and mouth. Flexing his sore jaw for a moment, Push then raised up so he could rim the circle of muscle concealed by Wrath's pale glutes. Wrath opened his legs wide to give Push access.

Push had always liked rimming, provided the man he was with understood basic hygiene. After a day of chasing bad guys and a night of attacks by aliens and robot monsters, Push knew Wrath's ass would not smell fresh like the morning sun. That should have been a turnoff by itself, but Wrath's enthusiasm urged Push forward.

The tang of sweat clung to the crevice, but there were surprisingly no unfamiliar tastes or odors, so Push dove in with no more thought. Wrath was busy stroking Push's cock as he alternately spat and applied his tongue to Push's asshole. When Push felt a finger, he rose in shock.

"That wasn't—" he started to say, before Wrath's finger hit his prostate.

Shocks went through Push like waves. Wrath's finger was warm, far warmer than it should have been or had any right to be. Somewhere amid his haze, Push realized the man must have been using his control over fire to add stimulation to Push's insides. The inside of his body past the sphincter felt like a sauna. The heat spread through Push, not enough to do damage but more than enough to melt away whatever resistance there was before.

Wrath kept twisting the finger around, adding another to it while heating the sphincter ring so that it relaxed much easier. When the third one went in, Push felt his cock lunge. At first, he feared he had cum all over Wrath's long hair. Looking up, Push realized his cock was leaking precum like a faucet. Drops rolled down the shaft like rain. Wrath ignored it for a moment, so intent was he on his task.

Finally, Push felt Wrath move. His head was swimming, and his vision had gone blurry moments before. Feeling Wrath lift his body forced Push to control himself. Slowing his breath, which had been matching the speed of his heart for a while now, Push rose and focused to where he could see somewhat clearly. Wrath was crouched between his legs, tearing something from a small black packet.

Push realized what Wrath was doing as the latex material was rolled expertly over the man's big dick. As Push opened his mouth to speak, he felt another surge go through him. It was then that he realized Wrath had kept at least one finger inside Push's asshole on the prostate nut. The flare of heat that went through Push silenced any remaining protest. When Wrath placed the tip of his dick at Push's entrance, their eyes met. Wrath hesitated then, leaving the decision up to Push, who willingly spread his legs wide to give the man better access.

Wrath needed no further invitation.

The head of Wrath's cock broke past Push's anal ring easily. Push had been cringing, waiting impatiently and fearfully for the intrusive feeling. When it slid in, his eyes popped open, and a gasp escaped from his throat. Wrath's powers had loosened the muscle to where Push's body accepted him with no hesitation.

The thickness still took a moment to adjust to. By the time Wrath had sheathed himself fully, the pain was all but a memory. Nothing was left for Push to feel but a sense of fullness and the amazing heat pulsating from deep inside, where Wrath's cock was lodged. The sensation almost sent Push over the edge right away. Clamping down, Push forced himself back. Whatever happened, he didn't want this to be over too fast for either of them.

Then Wrath started moving, and Push realized clenching so tightly only made things worse for them both. Wrath groaned, letting Push know how tight he was, and Push released slightly, giving Wrath more room to work.

They began moving together like an old habit, like practiced lovers. The strength and power, not to mention the familiarity, left Push breathless. Wrath's eyes only left Push's face when he leaned farther down to peck kisses in a row across Push's chest. Each one seared Push, making him hiss. Reaching out, Push locked both arms around Wrath's shoulder blades, where he remembered the two circle tattoos were.

At the same time, Push squeezed Wrath's lower half with his legs, forcing Wrath to fuck him deeper. The very depths of Push's inner channel were being penetrated now. It should have been excruciating. It should have been agony.

Push never wanted the feeling to stop.

Their bodies were soaked, drenching the already ruined upholstery, or what little remained of it after the explosion. Thinking of that made Push realize his balls were tightening up. He wanted to cry out, to warn Wrath to slow down, but couldn't form words in time. When his nuts unloaded, the spray of cum painted Push and Wrath both, splattering their chests with seed.

Wrath gave one hard shove into Push. Push closed his eyes, thinking that Wrath was cumming into the latex sheath keeping their flesh separated. When he opened his eyes, Wrath was stuck in a push-up position above him, eyes shut and straining as though in pain.

"Fuck!" Wrath cried out.

Push realized what was happening and pulled Wrath in deeper with his legs. "Don't hold back," he demanded, hoping to force Wrath's cum out of him. "Do it!"

"Can't!" Wrath hissed, panting. "Not yet!"

Push felt Wrath jerk out of him. The warm air burned against his gaping hole for a moment. Then Wrath seized Push in both arms and slung his body over the back of the couch. Push opened his mouth to object to being manhandled but stopped when he felt Wrath's cock at his entrance again. Push bit his lower lip to keep from moaning too loudly as Wrath forced his way back in.

Wrath's movements were rougher now. Push started to grunt as each powerful slam of Wrath's hips forced him into the upholstery. Wrath was fucking him with a fury now. Each thrust sent shockwaves of heat and rage through Push's smaller body. It was painful, but Push couldn't object. Even the pain felt good. It was making him boil over.

When Push felt his nuts draw up, the grunts coming out of his mouth intensified. Cum boiled out of his balls down the length of his shaft and sprayed the seat underneath them. As volley after volley of his cum splashed out, Push began to howl.

Wrath's hand clapped down over Push's mouth, but this couldn't silence him. The more Wrath fucked him, the louder he became, until Wrath was roaring with him. Their screams mixed together as Wrath jackhammered Push's asshole to his own climax, which caused the condom Wrath wore to flood. Push felt the latex fill until droplets splashed out onto his and Wrath's thighs.

Wrath's weight came crashing down on top of Push as the bigger man's orgasm slowly subsided. Despite this, Wrath continued moving in and out of Push, as if unable to stop. Push took in a deep gasp of air as Wrath's hand moved away from his mouth at last. Slowly, Wrath cradled Push in both arms, squeezing them tighter together even as Wrath's body continued to bear down on Push. It felt like Push was being absorbed into Wrath. Still, Wrath kept moving in and out until his cock finally softened enough to fall out along with the contents of the soaked condom.

Push heard Wrath whisper one word over and over again. It should have chilled him to the bone, but it didn't. The guilt he expected never came either. Instead, Push felt himself tingle as his brain absorbed what Wrath was saying.

"Mine."

CHAPTER
NINE

"MY LEGS are killing me."

It was the first thing Push had said for several minutes, if not longer. "How much farther do you think it is?"

Wrath had been quiet the whole time. The whole journey back, in fact, had been made in relative silence, which unnerved Push. Since the hovercraft was completely blown to pieces, along with their walkie-talkies, which they'd apparently left inside it, Push and Wrath were forced to make the trip back into town via the railroad tracks on foot. They'd cleaned each other off as best they could under the circumstances, speaking as little as possible, and dressed themselves in silence.

As they'd begun their trek following the train tracks, however, Wrath had reached out and taken Push by the hand. The gesture had caught him off guard, but Push hadn't pulled away. They'd stayed hand in hand together for most of the way, not speaking, but not avoiding each other either. Only as they neared the urban border of Shove Point did Wrath let go of Push's hand and begin moving away. The gap between them spoke volumes, but Push couldn't bring himself to fill it with vapid words. They were standing in the eye of a storm together and both knew it.

Push was confused, more so than he remembered feeling before. He should have been furious with himself, with Wrath, at himself and the ex-con for what they'd done. Push hadn't even tried to stop Wrath. It was the heat of the moment, or at least that was the excuse he was trying out on himself now. They'd almost died continuously for what felt like half the night. Then they were alive, and Wrath had been kissing him.

Everything afterward was a whirlwind of hands, skin, and sensation for Push. Thinking about it made Push's throat constrict and dry out.

"It's quiet." Wrath spoke, breaking the silence at last.

Push had to watch himself so he didn't trip. "I know," he replied, unsure of what else to say and feeling pissed all of a sudden for being so out of sorts with himself.

"I didn't mean that in a good way," Wrath said scathingly, cutting a sharp look over at Push. "We were invaded by aliens less than twenty-four hours ago. How can the town be this quiet?"

Every single nerve ending in Push's body went on high alert all at once.

"Something's happened," Wrath said, echoing Push's unvoiced thoughts. "I don't know what, but if people are being this calm…."

"We need to find the others," Push said. "Fast."

"No phones," Wrath said, and it sounded like he was rattling off a list to himself. "No land lines and no walkie-talkies."

"I know," Push said, feeling furious with himself for several reasons. "Shit!"

"It looks like we walk," Wrath finished, "at least until we come across a patrol car. Assuming they feel like giving us a lift."

"Where to?" Push swore under his breath the minute he spoke. "Which is closer?" he asked, looking around at the deserted street. "The police station or the house?"

"House," Wrath replied, not hesitating. "That way."

Wrath pointed ahead at a small street leading down toward what looked like a lumberyard. "If we go that way and turn right uphill, we'll be near the neighborhood in a few blocks or so, I think."

"Good."

It was hard to tell because of the force field, but Push thought the sun might be getting ready to break over the tree line beyond the town. The barrier gave off a green glow, tinting everything and bathing it in a sort of eerie dusk. Still, the town seemed brighter now than it had when they were coming down the tracks toward it.

Push stared at the stretch of road in front of them a moment before letting out a tired, almost defeated sigh.

"Let's go," he said, resigned to his fate.

The silence came back, stronger and more forceful than before. It felt like the lack of noise was urging Push forward. It gave him a bad feeling on top of the guilt that had finally started scratching lightly at his guts. He was going to regret everything very soon. The minute he saw Scratch's face, the world would end.

Never mind the aliens or the giant robots. He'd wanted Scratch for years, had beaten himself senseless on the inside for pining over a straight guy. Push had known Scratch would never feel the same way for him, but then remarkably, Scratch had.

Push had just had sex with Wrath.

It was the heat of the moment. They'd been about to die. Push thought they were dead men for sure. In the back of his mind, somewhere in a dark corner he hadn't bothered looking at, Push had worried Wrath would abandon him when the situation got rough. Wrath had been a soldier the whole time, however, a first-class trooper.

When the moment struck, something inside Push had shut down. Every last moral fiber he possessed went flying out the proverbial window. He'd survived. They had both survived, and the riptide of lust that Push had been holding back inside of himself broke free. Wrath had been all over him....

Push sighed. The guilt was back again.

It wouldn't work. He'd been snooping around in the crevices of his own heart the whole time, hoping to find something, a tiny scrap that might absolve him. No matter what, he'd never fought back or said no. Wrath hadn't assaulted him at all. Push had welcomed the man with open arms and taken each and every inch into him.

It had felt good. For the moment, that was the worst part. As guilty as he felt, Push couldn't stop thinking about how good it had felt to be taken over by Wrath, to have Wrath dominate him so completely. Worse yet, he wanted it all over again. Push's erection was straining his spandex tights now in a painful way. There was no way Wrath couldn't see, so long as he bothered to look Push's way. Push had been avoiding looking at Wrath, but now he recalled once again Wrath's empathic abilities. Wrath could feel everything going on inside of Push.

It should have made Push angry, and a spark flared for a brief instant. Push snuffed it out fast, though. He couldn't force total responsibility for something onto the man next to him. Wrath held far less guilt than Push did, at least as far as Push was concerned. Worse, Wrath had been a hero today. He deserved a parade, not ridicule.

Push was so fucked, and he knew it. The aliens could blow them up at any time, but for him, the world was already over.

Looking up, determined to at least face his doom with his head held less low to the ground, Push saw that they had reached the street where the house was located.

There was more light now, even if it was tinted the green color of sick. This cast the street in a strange, eerie fog of lime light that was hard to look at for long periods. Push felt his stomach twist into fresh new knots at the sound of his footsteps echoing over the asphalt. The closer they approached the house in silence together, the greater the dread that choked Push's throat.

By the time they had reached the front door, Push was ready to collapse. He felt overwhelmed, exhausted, and in need of about a year's worth of sleep. Bleary-eyed, Push pressed the doorbell and waited impatiently for someone to answer. He was half expecting Scratch to yank the door open from the other side, wide-eyed with fury and ready to make all kinds of accusations.

Instead, it was Wiccan Witch who eased the entrance open quietly. Her eyes widened for a moment at the sight of them, but she wasted no time in stepping aside so they could walk through.

"The others are still out," she said in a soft tone. "Where have you both been, though? Everyone has been trying to—"

"Metalsects," Wrath interrupted, speaking for the first time in a while. "They chased us through town and out to the border where the force field is. We trashed them, but the hovercraft got blown up along with our walkie-talkies. That's why we didn't call."

Wiccan Witch looked worriedly from Wrath to Push. "Oh my Goddess," she whispered. "I'm so sorry. How did you get back here?"

"We walked," Push answered in a normal tone, which sounded louder next to Wiccan Witch's hushed voice. "Why are you whispering?"

"The baby," Wiccan Witch answered, nodding back toward the far end of the house. "He had a rough night, at least for the first half. I didn't want to wake him."

Push had completely forgotten about the alien baby that was currently sharing a roof with them. Now that he thought on it, Wiccan Witch looked tired, like she hadn't slept for very long.

"How have you been?" Push asked, hoping she knew he was sincere despite the flat tone of his voice. "We couldn't make contact after the hovercraft blew up."

"I'm fine," Wiccan Witch assured him tenderly. "Thanks for asking, but I'll be all right. It's you two I'm worried about."

Push watched as Wiccan Witch brushed Wrath's arm lightly. "We're tired," Wrath replied, giving her hand a gentle squeeze. "That's all."

"Go get some rest," she ordered, leaving no room in her voice for arguments. "The others are still out. Actually, I was going to go look for you if no one found anything. Scarlet Queen said something about wanting to change shifts with me later. If you guys are willing to hold the fort down for a bit, I'll go out and relieve her so she can take a break."

"We'll take care of junior," Wrath said simply, giving Wiccan Witch a nod of reassurance.

"He's a good boy," Wiccan Witch said, looking over to Push. "You shouldn't have a problem getting some rest while he's asleep."

"Right," said Push, at a loss for any other response.

Wiccan Witch smiled sympathetically at Push before pointing him toward his room. "Sleep," she commanded tenderly. "I'll come soon."

"When you do," Wrath said, stopping her before she moved for the door. "When this is over, I have something to tell you."

Push hadn't taken a step toward his room, having stood there the whole time. Much as he felt like a Peeping Tom for continuing to watch, he couldn't look away. His brain was having trouble connecting the dots, so to speak.

Wiccan Witch, however, only nodded at Wrath's statement before giving Push one last glance. Then with a wave, as though she were running an errand, Wiccan Witch left, the door shutting gently behind her.

The sound was enough to snap Push out of it. Vividly, he was aware that Wrath was the only other person in the room with him. Forcing his feet to move, Push dragged himself through the living room and kitchen, down the short hallway to his bedroom. Once there, he collapsed across the covers, not bothering to undress or take his boots off.

He couldn't sleep. He had to get some sleep, but his mind was racing. Everything was different now. They had been invaded, and it was on his shoulders to fix everything.

They might die. They would all die.

Everything had turned to black.

It took several moments more before Push realized he'd already faded to unconsciousness. That was the last thought to echo in his mind before the darkness claimed him.

PUSH HAD no idea how long he slept. When his eyes snapped open, he found himself staring at an empty pillow. Confusion wracked his brain. He'd been having nightmares of all sorts, too many to keep them straight, but Push could distinctly remember falling asleep in a different position. The fact that this had stuck in his brain so easily felt weird, but there wasn't time to dwell on it.

Push was also under the covers. He definitely didn't remember falling asleep underneath them. Moreover, he was also naked.

Someone had come in while Push was out and tucked him in. Deciding it was Scratch, Push felt a surging need to be with his man. Ignoring the aches, pains, stiffness, and overall exhaustion in his body, Push dragged himself over to the edge of the bed and swung his feet onto the floor. As he did, the doorbell rang.

Sighing, Push stood up, grabbed a dirty pair of boxers off the floor, and slipped into them. The doorbell rang again as Push stumbled wearily down the foyer and around the corner through the living room.

However, upon opening the front door, Push saw there was no one standing outside. Blinking, Push looked around the front yard and spotted the back of a young girl.

There was a note stuck to the door. Push brushed the sleep out of his eyes before pulling the note down. Looking out across the yard at the disappearing figure, Push happened to catch sight of the girl's face when she turned and looked halfway back around.

"Sally," he said aloud, remembering the name of their landlord's daughter.

Push considered calling the girl back, but she'd already put considerable distance between herself and the house. That, Push noted, and she seemed in a hurry to get wherever she was going. Evidently, there were people expecting her, and she had most likely been instructed to return right away. Thinking this, Push pulled the Post-it note that had been used to stick the first note to the door and scanned the scribbled writing.

"They asked me to bring this to you" was all it read.

Push opened the folded note and immediately recognized Scratch's handwriting.

"At the sheriff's station getting some rest. Wiccan Witch told me about the fight and the hovercraft. Wish I was with you.—hugs—I love you."

Push clutched the note tightly as a hundred thoughts raced through his mind. He remembered the way it had felt when Scratch and he first became friends. He remembered being out by the tracks after the metalsects were destroyed. He could remember how amazing it had felt being with Scratch for the first time. He could remember Wrath kissing him and the way his skin had tingled when Wrath's hands touched him.

He could remember how hard he'd cum while Wrath was fucking him.

Push dropped both pieces of paper and ran back inside. Something wet landed on his hand as he reached out to shut the door behind him. It took Push a moment to work out that he was crying.

Scratch had said he loved Push. Push had told Scratch the same thing, and now they were done. Scratch hadn't even heard the truth from him yet, but it would be over for certain.

Feeling half-dead on the inside, Push carelessly dropped the Blackberry back on top of the nightstand next to his bed and stood up. He needed to stop crying and shower. Aliens had invaded Earth and encased Shove Point in a force field. Superheroes did not reek of body odor or cry over their relationship screwups during a crisis.

It was undignified.

"Batman would never cry over breaking up with Vicky Vale while the Joker was rampaging through Gotham," Push muttered, wincing as he staggered toward the bathroom. "Batman doesn't whine about being stiff and sore after staying up all night, either."

Push winced as the bottoms of his feet touched the cold tub lining. Forgoing the cold completely, he reached down and turned the hot water nozzle all the way. The faucet let out a feeble wheeze, coughed out a few spurts of icy cold water, then gurgled.

"Fuck!" Push swore.

Grabbing a towel and securing it, Push stormed out of the bathroom and through his room for the door. Once out of the small hallway, he looked around for signs of someone else. There was a noise in the back. Push stomped through the kitchen toward it. He wasn't concerned with who it was for the moment. All that mattered was him getting the chance to vent.

The world could end if it wanted to, but dammit, he needed a hot shower!

Rounding the turn at the end of the hall, Push came to the room that had been Scratch's. Having come closer to the sounds, Push realized someone was singing. He didn't recognize the tune, but it was enough to get him to slow down. Completing the turn, Push came to the opened door that was Scratch's temporary lodging and found Wrath standing with the space baby slung over one shoulder.

The kid, or Xavier as Wrath had insisted on naming him, opened his eyes and smiled at the sight of Push. Push gulped as the baby let out a delighted coo, which caused Wrath to swing around sharply.

"Oh, it's you," Wrath said. "I heard the doorbell a minute ago. Was it the cops again?"

Push paused, forgetting why he was roaring through the house in nothing but a towel. The sight of Wrath tickling the space kid and giving it Eskimo kisses made him lose his train of thought.

"The cops were here?" Push asked instead, still dumbfounded by what he was bearing witness to.

"A little while ago," Wrath replied, not looking up. "They wanted to come in. I was worried one of them would hear Xavier, but he stayed quiet the whole time."

Xavier gave a laugh, like he knew exactly what Wrath was referring to.

"What did they want?" Push wondered, stepping forward tentatively.

"Mostly wondering where you were," Wrath said, finally looking up at Push with a somewhat strained look on his face. "I explained about the big metalsect fight and how we needed a quick nap to recharge. The others are camping out at the sheriff's department for right now."

Push started to say he was already aware of this but snapped his mouth shut before Scratch's name could come up. Something boiled inside of Push, but he was determined not to let it out right now.

"Wiccan Witch is there too," Wrath was saying. "We've got command of Spandex Central for the time being."

Push blinked. "What?"

"That's what the cop that came by called this place," Wrath said, shrugging. "Why not?"

The fact that the local authorities were referring to their temporary home as Spandex Central was the least of Push's worries, so he set the matter aside.

"He's been such a good boy," Wrath said, tickling Xavier under the chin.

Push watched, still befuddled by the sight, as Xavier kicked happily and giggled. When he looked up at Wrath, the pyrokinetic was watching him carefully.

"You're thinking of giving him back, aren't you?"

Wrath's voice was careful. It was not a good sign. Push could hear the tension in Wrath's voice, but it was the way the other man's hands clenched slightly that made him so uncomfortable. The look in Wrath's eyes was unmistakable.

If Push tried to take Xavier away for any reason, Wrath would fight him.

"We can't keep him," Push tried, knowing full well that reasoning with Wrath would likely go nowhere. "Whether they mean to do him harm or not, Xavier is their baby."

"Then why did they toss him into a space carriage and send him flying into a plane?"

Push paused, knowing that was a valid statement. "They've got us on the run," he said instead, not answering Wrath. "Giving the kid back could solve all our problems. For all we know, this kid is important to them. They've at least sealed the town off. That's probably because they're looking for him."

Wrath said nothing, but the look on his face told Push that the matter was far from settled. "People are terrified, Wrath," Push said, still hoping to make the man see reason. "People are dead because of this."

The kid, Xavier, had gone completely quiet now. It was unnerving, but more so was the way his eyes locked onto Push without moving.

"I know you hate this place," Push continued, refusing to let himself be psyched out by an infant, even an alien one. "Is that why you're doing this?"

Wrath frowned but softened as Xavier looked up at him. "I can't explain it," Wrath said, letting out a sigh that ruffled the locks of black hair curling out of Xavier's head. "Since we took him out of that pod, I've felt something."

Push almost scowled. "That's it?" he wondered in a disdainful tone. "Your 'Papa Bear' instincts have kicked in. Is that it?"

Wrath and, to Push's surprise, Xavier both stared. "It's not that," Wrath said, and it sounded to Push like he'd struck a tender nerve with his words.

"Look, I'm sorry," Push interjected quickly. "I'm as exhausted as everyone else is, and to top it off, the shower water isn't working."

"There isn't any working water all over town." Wrath's expression shifted slightly as he spoke. "Sorry, I thought you must have heard that as well. The aliens attacked the water plant while we were out. The whole town is without water or power."

A throbbing pain began in the spot between Push's eyes and spread across his forehead. "Goddamn, how can this get worse?" he cursed at himself. "We don't have power. We don't have water. I can't even wash off. The rest of the team has been running around while I was sleeping, and I have no idea...."

Push caught himself and stopped before he could rant any further.

"I know," Wrath said. "The world might come to an end, and there's little any one of us can do at the moment to keep that from happening. We're all feeling the pressure, Push."

"It's different." Push almost shouted those words but managed to hold back enough that they only came out louder than necessary. "I'm the one in charge here. I'm supposed to lead everyone, to be an example for them. Instead, I almost get us killed, cause Trixter's hovercraft to blow up, and then...."

Push couldn't finish that sentence, but he didn't have to. Wrath did it for him.

"Then," Wrath concluded, "we made love out in the woods before the sun rose."

Push's eyes flashed with rage, and his nostrils flared. "That was not what happened," he hissed. "You and I didn't do anything.... We just...."

"Fucked?" Wrath offered, not bothering to shield his language in front of the child. "It didn't feel that way to me. Maybe we weren't tender about it, but there was some emotion behind the act. Believe me, I would know."

At that moment, Push wanted more than anything to choke the life right out of Wrath's body. "Why?" he asked instead. "Was it some kind of game you were playing with me?"

Wrath sighed and set Xavier down on the bed. Apparently, Wiccan Witch had fashioned a kind of makeshift cradle for the baby out of blankets, folding them into a bowl-like shape so Xavier couldn't roll off the adult-sized bed.

"Come on," Wrath said, once he'd gotten the baby settled. "This isn't a conversation I'd care to have in front of the child."

Push stepped aside to let Wrath leave first, then followed after him. Reaching for the door, he took one last look at the child nestled amid the folded blankets while Wrath waited impatiently outside. Hearing Wrath clear his throat, Push stepped out into the hallway, closing the door completely behind him.

"Okay," Push said, no longer as self-assured or confident as he had expected himself to be. "I guess we ought to talk, or—"

"Or what?" Wrath challenged, moving toward Push. "Something more like this?"

Push tensed as Wrath seized his jaw with one hand. Their mouths met, and whatever resistance Push had been prepared to show evaporated. Wrath didn't move, holding them together while Push felt the strength leave his knees again.

Something welled up inside Push, urging him to respond, but Wrath jerked away before Push could make a move of his own.

"I want to," he said breathlessly, almost a gasp. "You don't know how much I want to."

Push blinked. "What?"

"You," Wrath growled, glaring. "I've wanted you from the start. Even knowing how Scratch felt the same way about you as you did about him didn't stop me from wanting to be with you. I'd never fallen for anybody quite like that before. Not that fast, and not all at the same time."

Push inhaled slowly and deeply, more to steady himself than anything. "Then why…," he tried, only to fumble his words. "Why did you… what about when I caught you and Scratch together?"

Wrath scowled and jerked away, ashamed. "It sounds so stupid now," he muttered. "I just wanted to do something good."

Push didn't know what to say or how that related to what they were talking about, but he bit down on the urge to speak again so soon. Wrath, it seemed, wasn't done.

"I almost ran," Wrath went on. "When that transport taking me to Chicago was attacked, I almost took off for New Orleans. There was nothing back there for me, though, and even if I went, it wouldn't be the same. I figured I could start over."

Push watched as Wrath clenched his hands into fists. "But I don't know how to be a good person," Wrath whispered. "I don't know how to be a hero. I've been bad from the start, so I was told."

Finally, their eyes met. Push didn't need to be empathic in that moment to know Wrath was teetering on the edge of something horrific and painful. It made him grimace on the inside to see what was going on behind Wrath's eyes.

"So I thought I'd give you two a little nudge," said Wrath, as though confessing something terrible. "You'd be surprised. Sometimes, all people need is to get mad enough to do what they've wanted to do all along. Even though I wanted it to be you and me, I sent him running after you that night."

Push was too floored to speak.

"So now you're with him," Wrath continued, resigned. "And I'm with Wiccan Witch."

Something about Wrath's tone struck a nerve. "You don't sound thrilled," Push snapped at him irritably. "What's wrong with Wiccan Witch?"

"Nothing," Wrath answered at once, shrugging. "She's sweet, and she seems to get who I am. Truth be told, if I wasn't hung up on you so bad, there would be no problem."

That made Push hesitate.

"She wouldn't be angry about what happened between us," Wrath went on, ignoring Push's obvious sudden discomfort. "Wiccan Witch doesn't believe in monogamy. So long as people are honest with one another, she's happy to share."

Try as he might, Push was having a hard time keeping up with Wrath's train of thought, even though he himself felt like the answer was obvious.

"So," Push tried, feeling frustrated. "What's the real problem, then?"

Wrath looked at him. "The real problem is," he stated, "that you are with Scratch, and Scratch won't think very highly on the idea of sharing you with me."

CHAPTER
TEN

PUSH DIDN'T know how to argue against Wrath's logic. He wasn't entirely certain he should, for that matter. Push didn't want to be in a relationship with two men at the same time. The idea alone sounded absurd to him. Wrath was with Wiccan Witch, and he finally had Scratch. There was no more room in his life for another boyfriend, much less Wrath, and they'd already found the people they belonged with anyway.

Hadn't Wrath just stated that he felt like Wiccan Witch understood him?

Push started to speak, hoping he came up with something that wasn't too vapid or blunt while his mouth hung open. Before a sound came out, Push was interrupted by a loud, high-pitched beeping sound.

"What was that?" he asked, hoping he didn't sound too grateful for the interruption.

"It came from Trixter's room," Wrath said, nodding at the door that was behind Push at the end of the hall.

Push turned around and noticed the door just a step or two away was shut. The sound came again, and curiosity got the better of him.

"He's been known to leave stuff on," Push said, justifying his meddling in Trixter's privacy. "It may be something important."

"You don't have to explain it to me," Wrath retorted somewhat gently, following after Push, who was easing the door open slowly. "I used to be a criminal. Invading people's privacy is par for the course in that occupation."

Push tuned Wrath out and looked around inside the small bedroom. Trixter had crammed every last available bit of space with equipment. At first, there was so much stuff that Push didn't know where to begin looking. Then the sound came yet again, and Push's eyes landed on a laptop on the corner of the bed.

"He must have a message," Push said, stepping through the tightly packed room.

"I thought the power was gone," Wrath said curiously. "How can any of this stuff still work?"

"Trixter keeps backup power cells in case something like a power failure happens while he's working," Push replied, reaching the laptop. "He's lost valuable data that way."

Push opened the laptop and spotted a small icon on the toolbar flashing on and off. Bringing the mouse around, Push gave the icon a click and saw it was a video message program. Push's jaw fell as the figure on the screen came into view.

"It's about time," Margaret Liu shouted, glaring up at him from her camera. "I was beginning to think there was nobody left connected in that stupid hick town."

"Margaret?" Push asked, once his jaw had drawn back up. "You're alive?"

"Push?" Margaret squinted at her screen. "Oh, thank God it's you. I was worried some dumbass redneck was going to luck out and pick up."

"Where are you?" Push demanded. "Are you all right? Did you know that you're listed as dead? What's going on right now? We're—"

"I know," Margaret said forcefully. "Believe me, I know all about it. Things have been nothing but disastrous since the attack on the Association headquarters. I managed to slip away, but things have gotten worse since that big bubble thing appeared over Shove Point."

"All communications inside the town have been shut off," Wrath said, taking a seat on the bed beside Push. "There is no power or water, and the phones aren't working."

Margaret looked closer. "Ah, Wrath," she said, recognizing him. "Nice costume."

"Thank you," Wrath replied.

"How bad is it?" Push demanded, wanting to get back on topic.

Margaret let out a long, heavy sigh. "Bad," she stated flatly. "It isn't just Shove Point. The hostiles, as they're being referred to for right now, have invaded Earth. They've taken a number of major cities across the globe, but this is the interesting part. The big metropolises I can understand, but Shove Point is the only nonmajor city with a dome over it."

Push stiffened.

"The government assumes that there must be something there the aliens need," Margaret was saying, oblivious to Push's mood shift. "At the moment, though, things are stretched pretty thin. There's talk of having the military go down there, but right now, it's all anyone can do to hold things together."

"So it's official," Push said, feeling the weight crush him. "We're at war."

"Sure looks that way," Margaret retorted dryly.

"How are you able to communicate with us?" Wrath asked curiously. "I didn't think any signals could penetrate the force field surrounding Shove Point."

"They can't," Margaret replied. "Not officially, at least. When the Association building in Chicago went down, I hid out in one of the warehouses where we keep experimental equipment. Some of it has come in pretty handy. I've been working on trying to get signals through. So far, you're the only ones to reply."

"What do we do?" Push asked, not bothering to hide the desperation in his voice. "What about the Cape Cabinet?"

"They're meeting at the White House," said Margaret, smirking sourly. "Sorry, but it looks like we're on our own for now."

Push squared his shoulders and let out a deep breath. "We're here," he declared. "And we're all available. Besides Wrath and myself, there's Scratch, Wiccan Witch, Scarlet Queen, Professor Trixter, and two more that joined us recently. It's the eight of us plus the local police force."

"Then you're in for the fight of your lives," Margaret said grimly. "I hope you're all up for it."

"No one said we weren't," Wrath replied. "What can we do to help?"

"A lot, actually." Margaret's face vanished for a moment as she reached for something off-screen. There was nothing behind her but a blank space. Wherever she was, Push reasoned it was a very good hiding place.

"Sorry," Margaret said in a rush upon returning. "Everything here is so disorganized. I feel like I'm back at the office."

That made Push smile in spite of himself.

"For the moment, the best thing you can do is get everyone organized," she went on. "I'll send you the data on the aliens that I've gathered as we go along. There's undoubtedly a lot that you can do with it since you're behind enemy lines. If the locals are willing to act as soldiers, you may have a fighting chance. The plan I've conceived so far would work better with some kind of army backing you guys."

Wrath stood up. "I'm going to message the others on the walkie-talkie," he told Push, who glanced away from the screen briefly. "They need to be here for this."

"I agree," said Margaret from her end.

"Right," Push concurred. "So let's get to work."

Push could hear Wrath's voice distantly from the kitchen but tuned it out for the moment as Margaret adjusted her camera.

"There," she said. "That's better. Now, I need to assess everything you and the other heroes have at your disposal right now. Anything you have that can be used against the aliens, even if it doesn't seem important, needs to be cataloged so we can—"

"Push!" Wrath's voice cut Margaret off as he came around the corner into view. "There's trouble."

"What?" Push asked, giving Wrath his full attention.

"What's happened?" Margaret asked on-screen, sounding surprised.

"I can't reach anyone through the walkie-talkie," Wrath said as he reentered the room. "No one at the station is responding."

Push hesitated. "It could be that they're asleep," he tried, "or that they left the walkie-talkie unattended."

"Do you really buy that?"

Push met Wrath's eyes and shook his head. "I'm sorry, Margaret," he said, putting the laptop aside as he got off the bed. "We have to check and make sure the others are all right."

"Go," she said. "I have to terminate this connection before the aliens discover it, but I'll try to contact you again soon."

Push was already making his way past Wrath and down the hall. "You might want to put some pants on, at least," Wrath advised, coming up behind him. "It's your call, but—"

Push cut him off. "I know," he said sharply. "Meet me outside in two minutes. I just need to grab my bo and some pants and shoes."

"Will do." Wrath took two steps before whirling back around. "What about Xavier? There's no one to watch him."

Push thought furiously for a moment. "He'll be okay," Push insisted, as much to himself as Wrath, "at least for an hour. Besides, this is a major emergency. He'll be as bad off as we are if the worst has happened."

"We can't leave a kid here alone," said Wrath insistently.

It sounded to Push like Wrath was gearing up for a fight, one they couldn't afford to have at the moment.

"We can't take him with us into a war zone either," Push pointed out. "There's no one we can call on right now to watch him. We don't have that kind of luxury in this town, Wrath. You know that better than I do."

Push ran to his room, leaving Wrath to hesitate a moment more before racing to the back.

"I'm going to check on him one last time," Wrath called out loudly. "Meet me outside."

Push didn't answer. In less than two minutes, he was fully dressed and armed. Push's uniform was lying at his feet on the carpet by the bed. He'd decided to forgo it in favor of civilian attire. One of the Association's classes involved their trainees knowing how to get in and out of spandex in under a minute, but Push felt time was of the essence.

That and it reeked.

Exiting the house, Push stopped short in the garage. Wrath was sitting inside a car Push didn't recognize, with the engine running.

"Where?" Push demanded, once he'd slammed the passenger door shut.

"Next door," Wrath replied, shifting the stick next to Push's knee into reverse.

"Okay," Push said, buckling himself into the passenger seat very quickly as the car rolled backward. "How?"

Wrath spun the car around, then shifted it into drive. As he took his hand off the stick shift, Wrath picked up a loose wire hanging down from underneath the wheel.

"Ever see the movie Gone in Sixty Seconds?" he asked, hitting the gas. "I managed this in forty-seven."

The sun was high in the sky, and the city streets were lit. Except for the places where there had been obvious fighting, Shove Point looked idyllic. Wrath wasn't giving Push a chance to enjoy the scenery, however. The car he'd stolen wove through the streets like a needle. Push held on for dear life and prayed to whoever was listening that they at least make it to the police station in one piece.

Not once did they see an alien or a metalsect. The roads were empty, and the people were nowhere in sight. All that changed when they roared down the highway past the police station.

It was on fire.

There were dead bodies.

In the middle of it all, though, standing out in the center of the parking lot in broad daylight, was Sloth.

Wrath didn't slow down. Turning the wheel sharply, the pyrokinetic brought the car up over the median and straight through the barrier. As they came to a sliding stop, Push undid his seat belt and jumped out the passenger door.

Sloth smirked when he caught sight of Push.

"No spandex?" he called out over the flames. "Seems kinda unconventional if you ask me."

"Where are they?" Push demanded, the fury in his voice thick.

Sloth laughed. "Don't worry," the albino assured Push in a deceptively calm tone. "I haven't killed anyone in your little clubhouse. I have my orders, after all."

Push stopped short at hearing this, but Wrath kept going. "I'd stay back if I were you," Sloth told Wrath warningly. "You don't—"

Push watched as Wrath raised both arms high overhead. "You're going to threaten me," Wrath said, his voice oddly quiet. "You're going to threaten me in front of a burning building?"

"Wait, Wrath!"

Push ran up to Wrath's side and gently held him back with one arm. "Sloth, what's the point of doing any of this?" Push demanded, giving the albino a hateful glare. "There are bigger problems here than any of us."

The flames from the ruined station behind them flared but remained where they were, content to feed on the building's remains. Sloth gave them a glance, smiling, before looking back to Push.

"You play pretend hero all you want," said Sloth, grinning as he pointed a fat, accusatory finger at Push. "This is about me getting what I came here for and getting out of this stinking town."

Sloth's eyes narrowed suddenly. "And I've got a gut intuition that the two of you know exactly where I can find it," he said coolly. "This whole rattrap of a town can burn if it has to. The bugs pointing death rays at us, whatever the fuck they're here for, can have the leftovers once I'm done. I'm getting my package and finishing my delivery."

"No." Wrath's voice was ice cold as he shoved Push away. "You're not," Wrath said, letting out a low growl following his words. "I'm through playing games. This is over, Sloth."

Sloth grinned. "Is it?" the muscled man challenged.

Fire exploded out of the burning building, filling the air over their heads and forming circles within circles. Wrath held his arms up again as the circles spun, centering themselves above where Sloth stood.

"Like I said," Wrath went on, a thread of leisurely enjoyment weaving through his words. "You shouldn't have done this in front of a burning building."

Sloth snorted derisively, ignoring the fire above him. Push noticed, however, a few beads of sweat dripping down the side of the man's head.

"You don't have the guts," Sloth called out dismissively. "I had to force you to make your first kill that time when we were—"

Wrath suddenly snapped one finger. Flames burst forth from the building directly behind where Sloth stood, enveloping him. Push's eyes widened in shock as the flames swallowed Sloth's body whole.

"Wrath, no!" he cried out, but it was too late.

Wrath brought both arms down, sending the rings of fire slamming into Sloth's body, which was already collapsing on the concrete. More ropes of flame reached out of the station, each one centering its attack on the spot where Sloth lay. In seconds, the spot on the concrete was a blazing pillar of fire. Wrath held both arms out in front of him now, pouring every last drop of concentration into the assault.

Push could only watch in horror as the man next to him burned Sloth to a crisp.

"You're right," Wrath said through gritted teeth.

"What?" Push asked, as though snapping out of a daze, before coming to his senses. "Wrath, that's enough! You're going to kill him."

"You did have to make me kill that first time," Wrath went on, ignoring Push completely even as Push tried to force his arms down. "But I've learned since then, and I know now the value of a sneak attack."

Push clenched his fists, took aim, and fired a telekinetic blast straight at Wrath, knocking him off his feet. Wrath rolled into the blow, coming back onto his feet in a crouching position using the momentum of Push's attack. Both men stared at one another as the flames in front of them died slightly.

"It didn't have to be this way, Wrath," Push snarled, feeling his rage boil over.

"We can't fight him and the invaders," Wrath countered, standing, "And we can't waste time trying to keep him locked up when he'll just break out again and cause more trouble."

"Maybe not," Push said, though saying so aloud killed a small part of him. "Maybe... you're right about that, but this isn't the answer."

"Yes, it is," Wrath retorted, though much quieter than before. "The problem isn't that this wasn't the answer. The problem is that you don't like it."

Wrath stepped forward. Push moved to fire another blast his way, but Wrath kept going, ignoring Push in favor of the burning police station.

"We have to find the others," said Wrath, his voice unsteady as he stared into the flames. "Sloth said they were alive, but we won't know for sure...."

Push waited, but Wrath never finished his sentence. "If that's the case," Wrath said instead. "It's just the two of us now."

The weight of those words struck Push like a blow to the head and the gut at the same time. "Scratch," he whispered, the gravity of everything finally settling in. "We have to find Scratch."

"We have to find everyone," Wrath countered angrily. "But yes," he added, softly, "Scratch. And Wiccan Witch."

Push started to charge for the building, but Wrath took hold of his arm. Using his free hand, Wrath extinguished the flames blanketing Sloth's corpse, gathering what remained up in one hand. Letting Push go, Wrath brought both palms together, cupping the fire and shaping it into a ball.

"Get the door," Wrath said. "I'll take care of the fire once we have a way in."

Push charged, stopping short of the entrance and thrusting both hands out. The entrance exploded inward, creating a backdraft that sent flames toward the spot where Push stood. Wrath was ready for them, however, and was suddenly at Push's back. Bringing the flames around them on both sides, Wrath then extended his arms and legs out, letting the fire bend and encircle his limbs.

"I'm fine," Wrath assured Push, though Push thought Wrath's voice sounded distorted slightly. "Let's go."

Wrath went in first, waving his arms back and forth with each step he took once they were past the main entrance. Each time Wrath fanned his arms, fire flew from them and blew across the flames eating at the floor. Both sets of flames extinguished, leaving a path for them to follow on.

"Careful," Wrath warned Push over the noise. "This place is filled with smoke, and the fire has most likely rendered it unstable."

Push coughed hard. "I noticed," he choked out forcibly. "I guess that means it's my turn, then. We need some ventilation."

Spotting several windows, Push began blasting them out with his telekinetic powers. The smoke poured out through the vacant spots in the walls, but it wasn't enough to clear the room. Wrath was still fanning the flames out using his powers, but there wasn't enough oxygen for both of them to breathe. Push didn't see how Wrath could stand breathing so much smoke, but there wasn't time to ask him.

Taking aim at the ceiling, Push took a chance and blasted a couple of holes in the roof. None of them were very big, but the risk of him bringing the place down was high. However, the smoke had to escape somehow, and they were running low on time. Push fired several more times, opening up more holes, which helped considerably. With the fire dying down thanks to Wrath, the smoke was beginning to clear.

"Where are they?" he shouted between coughs.

Wrath did not answer but waved his arms around widely, opening up a path to the holding cell area.

"Right," Push coughed out, breaking into a run.

The lack of clean air made running even that short a distance challenging, but Push forced his muscles to comply. Blasting the door off for the second time, Push raced through to the back area.

The others were resting inside a cell together. The sight made Push stop short despite time running out. All of them—Wiccan Witch, Scarlet Queen, Dixie Whistler, Statique, Professor Trixter, and Scratch—were stretched out along the floor. Sloth had arranged their unconscious bodies as though they were only sleeping. It didn't look to Push like they were seriously hurt, but the bizarre part was the small canisters of oxygen next to each one.

"The hell?" Push wondered, before snapping back to reality.

Questions would come later, after they'd gotten out of the burning police station. The door to the cell was unlocked, meaning all Push had to do was shove it aside and collect his teammates. Push hesitated a moment, worried about whether he should move them, especially with the oxygen masks covering all their faces.

"Are we done yet?" Wrath's voice echoed down the hall to Push. "I'd rather not stand around and wait for the ceiling to collapse on us."

"Give me a hand," Push called out, taking hold of Wiccan Witch, who was nearest to the door. Push could feel the steady pulse of her heart beneath his hand. "They all look all right, but they're unconscious."

Wrath came racing down the hall, his footsteps matching Push's heartbeat. "I got the fire put out," he said, coughing now. "Most of it, at least, but we shouldn't stick around. There's nothing left but dead bodies, and I think they were gone before Sloth set fire to the place."

"Come on," Push said, straining as he lifted Wiccan Witch up and passed her to Wrath. "Two at a time, if you can manage that much."

"Where did the oxygen tanks come from?" Wrath wondered, though he didn't hesitate to accept Wiccan Witch from Push, along with Scarlet Queen.

"No idea," Push replied, getting Scratch and Dixie Whistler next. "Don't much care either. Let's just be grateful for small favors."

As they were exiting the building, someone slammed into Push hard. Dazed, he let go of Scratch momentarily and raised one hand to attack. Sheriff Black was looking at Push with a wide-eyed expression of pure shock and horror.

"What happened?" he asked, reaching out to help Push catch Scratch before Scratch hit the ground.

"Sloth," Push replied, gasping. "Got out. Two more in the back still."

Sheriff Black didn't hesitate. The moment Push had a secure grip on Scratch again, he took off through the doors for the holding cell area. A few minutes later, Statique and Professor Trixter were being brought out by local officers.

It looked like only a handful of the police were there, judging by the number of police cars. Either they'd gotten suspicious by the lack of response on the walkie-talkie band or someone had spotted the smoke. Push didn't much care. It looked as though his team was all right. The oxygen had prevented them from suffering smoke inhalation, and to the best knowledge of the locals on hand, they'd merely been knocked out with tranquilizers.

Push was too grateful for the time being to care why.

Wrath, however, wasn't.

"Look at this," Wrath said, holding up a canister in front of Push, who was still feeling overwhelmed by everything.

"What?" Push asked, not the least bit interested.

"The label," Wrath said.

Push stared down at the label on the side of the canister that Wrath was holding in front of him. As his eyes adjusted, he saw what Wrath meant.

"This came from the local hospital," Wrath said, speaking aloud what Push had already put together. "Sloth was locked up along with Lust, so how did either of them get their hands on this?"

The pieces came together very quickly. "In the hospital before," Push said as adrenaline began creeping into his blood. "The time before, I mean. You sensed Envy in the hospital but couldn't pinpoint where he was."

"Envy is still in town," Wrath said. "That explains the use of drugs, but why spare them?"

"I don't know," Push said. It felt like those words were becoming a mantra. "The others, they can't go to that hospital. We have to take them back with us and let them recover at the house. It isn't safe anywhere else."

Wrath nodded his agreement. "We should probably have a code word or something to use so we know who it is we're talking to. It sounds cheesy, but Envy is remarkably adept at impersonating people, even those he hasn't known for very long."

"We should hurry up, then," Push said, his eyes suddenly drawn to the force field still hanging above their heads. "The rest of the Deadly Seven are still on the loose and we've got aliens to deal with."

Looking back down, Push caught Wrath watching Scratch's stirring body closely. "Cry havoc, then," Wrath said. "And let loose the dogs of war."

"An Emmy-award-winning performance."

Lust paused to run the tip of his tongue along the side of his knife while kicking his legs back and forth like a kid underneath the table he sat on. "I was totally convinced," Lust went on, smirking. "There's no way they didn't buy it."

"Shut up," Envy replied, shrugging out of the charred remains of his Sloth disguise. "You weren't even there."

Their voices echoed off the walls of the hospital basement room. Sloth, who was off to the side, away from Lust, leaning one shoulder against a wall, frowned.

"You sure they can't hear us?" he pressed. "We don't need any hospital personnel getting suspicious and checking this place out."

Lust laughed as the costume debris Envy had been wearing hit the tile floor. "I've been around you long enough to have gauged your acting skills," Lust countered gleefully, acting as though he hadn't heard Sloth speak. "I'm sure you knocked 'em dead. Literally."

Sloth struck Lust across the back of the head to silence him. "Enough," he ordered, before turning to Envy with a serious face.

"No one comes around this part of the hospital," Envy assured him, picking the ruined clothing up off the floor and dumping it into a nearby dirty clothes barrel. "We're clear."

Sloth nodded. "And they bought it?" he pressed, sounding anxious.

"They bought it," Envy said, his body filling the brown pants he was now slipping into. "As far as those 'heroes' know, you're a charred corpse that got carried off along with the rest of the dead we left in that parking lot. Speaking of which, I need to put on my Hamilton face and get upstairs before I'm missed."

"Good." Sloth nodded, letting out a relieved breath. "Killing so many was a risk, but I wasn't sure anything less would be enough to nudge our firebug over the edge."

"I still don't know about that little shit-faced punk," Lust growled menacingly, giving his knife a twirl. "Are you sure he'll come around?"

Envy was ignoring Lust and slipping into the white doctor's overcoat he wore as Hamilton. "My job's finished for now," he said. "How much longer before we can leave this cow-pie town, Sloth? Things have gotten too complicated."

Sloth scowled at Lust, who was balancing on the table's edge upside down on one hand.

"Wrath will come around," Sloth answered, speaking to Lust first. "Once the bugs are done with this place and he's realized the truth, he'll be begging for a spot with our new organization. As for the bugs, let 'em have this rathole."

"I'd just as soon knife the kid," Lust snarled, slamming his blade down through a nearby table as he dropped to his feet. "He's too unstable."

That made Envy give Lust a hard stare. "And you're the model of emotional stability?" he challenged. "Leave the kid alone. Otherwise, you'll end up flash fried to a crackly crisp like I would have been."

Envy turned to Sloth, who seemed to be less than pleased by the turn the conversation was taking. "Speaking of which, have you got any more of that flame-retardant gel? I'd like some more in case the kid figures out whose face I've been wearing."

Sloth shrugged. "You seem to be doing okay keeping his empathy fooled so far," the albino pointed out evasively. "Why get worried about it now?"

"Because there's an angry pyrokinetic running all over town thinking you're dead," Lust told Sloth irritably, pacing back and forth. "You're out of the picture as far as the punk kid's concerned, but he'll be looking for the rest of us. I say we get as much of the gel as there is and bathe ourselves in it."

"It's poisonous if you keep it on your skin for too long," Sloth replied. "And I'd rather not waste it."

Lust stopped dead in his tracks and shot Sloth a murderous stare. "So it's okay to use so long as somebody else is bailing your pasty ass out of danger, am I right?"

Sloth shoved himself away from the wall. In three strides, he was standing in front of Lust, who had jumped backward out of Sloth's reach.

"Keep talking," Sloth said warningly. "I'm in no mood to deal with you right now, Lust, so just keep talking. You can have your choice between the bug-eyed freaks or the kid who's wanted to charbroil your ass for years. Either way, it shuts you up, which works out fine for me."

Envy watched both men for a moment, then cleared his throat. "As entertaining as either option sounds," he began, "that brings something to mind that I've been curious about."

Sloth turned one eye toward Envy while keeping the other squarely on Lust.

"What do we do about the aliens?" Envy asked quickly. "No offense meant, but is leaving them alone really the best option?"

To Envy's surprise, Sloth actually laughed.

"Wow," Lust said, lowering the knife he'd been holding behind his back. "You actually got him to laugh. I think I may puke now."

"Hold it in," Sloth told Lust, still snickering. "We don't need a mess on the floor."

"Sorry, boss man," Envy said. "I'm afraid I just don't get the joke."

Sloth shook his head, giving Lust his back as he returned to his leaning spot on the wall next to the table. "There's plenty of time," Sloth told them. "The bug-faces won't be done with this town for a little while yet, which gives me room to maneuver. The heroes will be too busy fightin' the good fight to waste time looking for us, which puts our side in the clear. Really, the bug-faces couldn't have shown up at a better time."

"You sound pretty fucking cheery for somebody whose planet just got curb stomped all over by a bunch of freaks from space," Lust noted, giving Sloth a shrewd look. "What's really going on here?"

Sloth shrugged, his face turning thoughtful. "Maybe something," he said, "or maybe nothing. I won't say for sure. Not yet, anyway."

Envy waited in case Sloth planned on elaborating. When the big man kept quiet, Envy shrugged and went back to finishing his Hamilton ensemble.

"Keep your eyes and ears open," Sloth told him as he headed for the door. "Right now, information is what we need. Stay alert more than ever."

"Right," Lust jeered. "And don't prescribe Viagra to someone with a heart condition."

Envy opened his mouth to retort, but found himself cut off by a bloodcurdling shriek that reverberated off the walls of the room and out the door into the corridor beyond. All three men turned their eyes toward a figure resting on an old-fashioned hospital bed in a corner, surrounded by a pale sheet. Until now, they'd been ignoring the figure, pretending he wasn't there.

"I thought you said you put him under," Lust said to Envy, accusingly.

Envy shrugged. "Sorry about that," he said in an unconvincing tone of voice. "He does that every so often. Just push that red button on the control pad if he does it again within the next ten minutes. That should give him pleasant dreams."

Lust backed away from the sheeted figure even farther. "Again," he spat out viciously. "Why do we have to be down here with that thing? It gives me the heebie-jeebies."

Sloth didn't look that much more reassured. "Are you certain he won't be discovered?" he asked Envy. "No one's suspected anything?"

Envy shook his head with confidence. "This is a third-rate hospital in a hick town filled with personnel that, for the most part, didn't score high enough to get a job someplace better. They aren't going to notice."

Sloth nodded but didn't look convinced. Lust was still watching the sheet-covered figure in the corner while running a thumb back and forth across the hilt of his knife. Envy saw this and started to say something, but Sloth cut him off with a sharp glare.

Sloth shook his head and spoke again. "Are you sure his condition is stable now?" he pressed. "I'd hate to lose such a valuable asset, but if it means not waking up on the wrong end of those claws, he can be put down."

"That shouldn't be necessary," Envy replied, slowly easing his way out the door. "The metallic supplements I switched with his IV treatments placated the nanobots—"

"Microbots," Lust interjected snidely. "You said they were too large to be nanobots."

"Shut up," Sloth commanded.

"Whatever," Envy said, continuing. "They finally stopped eating his body from the inside out. With the metals to work with, his condition should have stabilized. He'll be ready for the front lines soon enough."

"So long as nobody finds him or any of us," Lust grumbled, putting his knife away for the moment. "I guess if none of 'em suspected us of bringing him down here right after we snatched the lowlife out of his hospital bed, they aren't gonna waste time now that those bug-faced freaks are running loose all over town."

"An astute observation, Lust," Envy complimented, before adding, "For once."

Lust turned and stuck his tongue out at Envy, who ignored him.

"He'll need a name," Sloth said, ignoring both men. "That's something the big boys upstairs will insist on. Something that reflects the times we live in, I think."

"Bloodblade!" Lust exclaimed, whipping both knives out and spinning them.

Envy gave Sloth a dry look before turning around and walking out the door. "I'll leave that up to you," he said. "Good luck."

Lust stayed quiet until the door closed behind Envy. "Whadaya think?" he demanded insistently.

Sloth smiled. "Things are going well," he said, bravely walking over to the concealed bed to push the red button Envy had indicated. "Everything is still on schedule. We just have to wait until those heroes finish their job. Either they die as martyrs trying to save everyone in this pathetic town, or they actually win and move the big project forward faster than we'd anticipated. Even if the unlikely happens, it works out fine for us."

Lust frowned. "No," he said, not moving anywhere near Sloth or the deformed figure that had once been Duane. "I mean, what do you think of the name? Too nineties antihero?"

Sloth looked back at Lust for a second before turning thoughtfully toward the unconscious Duane.

"It could work," Sloth admitted.

EPILOGUE

Hero Gaiden

Enigma

Biloxi, Mississippi

A NAME was hardly enough to go on.

"Richard Oakstone," Enigma read aloud on the thin slip of paper he'd been sent.

The man on the phone had sounded nervous, antsy. The call had come via a disposable phone, meaning it was somebody who didn't want to be found. Enigma had nearly hung up on the guy, but then the magic words had come up.

"'I'm with the Association.'"

That had gotten Enigma's attention. If someone in the Real-Life Superhero Association was in some kind of trouble and needed his particular expertise, Enigma wasn't about to turn them away. It was still suspicious. Enigma was no fool when it came to his job, but an Association member was like a fraternity brother in his eyes.

So he'd waited, and just like the stranger on the phone had promised, the packet arrived through the mail. From the condition of the manila envelope, it had been halfway around the world. Several return address stickers were layered one on top of the other in the upper left-hand corner, indicating that it had made several stops. His client hadn't wanted the contents found, obviously.

Most of it was just old photographs. One in particular was of a trio standing in front of a movie theater. The young man and woman stood close to each other, but Enigma found himself zeroing in on the older man's hand, which was resting on the young man's shoulder. It almost looked fatherly.

Almost, Enigma thought, but not quite.

The elder male's face had been circled. His face was in the rest of the photographs. The job was a missing persons' case. Enigma's client wanted the man found. Evidently, the stranger felt it was worth sending Enigma a twenty-thousand-dollar retainer.

The phone rang, and Enigma knew who it was before he answered it. The caller ID read the number as unlisted, meaning it was his mystery man.

"I got your packet in the mail," he said, forgoing any pleasantries. "You really didn't want this being found. Seems silly for a missing persons' case."

The line was silent for a moment. "How did you know it was me?" the man on the other line demanded, sounding frantic.

Enigma laughed. "I don't get many calls on my phone from untraceable numbers," he retorted in a caustic tone. "You're the first I've ever come by for as long as I've had this number. Unless Saint Nick was giving me a ring to apologize for not bringing me that bicycle I asked for when I was seven, my money was on it being you."

The man on the other line hesitated. "Dick," he said at last, all but forcing the word out. "You can call me Dick if you need to."

"Dick works, I guess," Enigma said, leaning back in his office chair. "Mind explaining to me why you need this guy found?"

Enigma could hear the man calling himself Dick swallow on the other end of the line. The sound of his breathing was picked up by the phone, indicating nervousness and apprehension.

"I need to know where he is," Dick said softly, as though afraid of being overheard. "I need to ask him something very important."

Enigma allowed the silence that followed to drag out for a moment. "Twenty grand is a lot of money to spend on finding somebody just so you can shoot the shit," he noted. "I don't do favors for crooks, buddy. If you're looking to find this guy so somebody else can break his legs, I'm afraid I'm gonna have to decline your generous—"

Dick didn't give him a chance to finish. "It isn't like that!" he shouted. "I don't want him hurt at all. I just…."

Enigma listened to the hurt in the man's words and contemplated the painful gasp that followed. Spotting a profile shot of the so-called Richard Oakstone lying on his desk, Enigma plucked the photograph up and studied it for a moment.

"How did it happen, Dick?" he asked gently. "I won't do a job unless I have all the facts, so you're gonna have to take the plunge and trust me."

Dick was silent again. "Nothing happened," he said cautiously, which made Enigma chuckle. "We just… had a fight, and then—"

"I wasn't talking about that," Enigma countered, cutting Dick off. "I saw the picture of the three of you in front of that big theater. The girl looked like a keeper, but the older guy's hand was on your shoulder the whole time."

Enigma waited while his words settled in. "She wasn't enough," he went on, taking advantage of the moment. "You must have cared about her, Dick, going by how tightly you were holding on to her, but it just wasn't enough. You wanted something more than what she was willing to give. Something that was standing just to the right of you on that particular night."

Dick swallowed loud enough for Enigma to hear. "You are good," Dick praised in a hollow voice. "I wasn't sure at first, but you saw right through it."

Enigma smiled sourly. "Never satisfied," he said, the words bitter in his mouth. "That's human nature for you, I guess. No matter how great you've got it, there's something you want that's just out of your reach."

Dick laughed, and it sounded to Enigma like the man was mocking him.

"You're a bitter old fart," Dick declared. "Just like the stories said. Maybe I should have gone to your partner instead."

Enigma scowled. "He's busy at the moment. I guess that leaves me to chase after the ghost of your ex-boyfriend, though I still want to know why you need me to hunt him down. If it isn't so the two of you can make nice, what other reason could there be?"

Dick didn't answer. Enigma thought he had hung up and was on the verge of doing the same when he heard shuffling in the background.

"I took a big risk contacting you," Dick hissed, like he was terrified of being overheard.

"That goes without saying," Enigma retorted. "Try telling me something I wasn't already aware of for once."

Dick made a noise, like halfway between a sigh and an angry grunt. "Fine," he spat out. "Richard Oakstone used to be the Midnight Owl."

Enigma waited, but Dick said nothing more. "Sorry, kid," he said. "You're gonna have to do better than that. The Association has something like four hundred members on its roster."

Dick actually laughed. "The Midnight Owl was never a member of the Real-Life Superhero Association," he said dryly. "Richard hated the Association."

Now Enigma was a bit more intrigued. "I guess it shouldn't surprise me that you haven't heard of him," Dick went on. "The Association was always doing their best to keep his activities quiet. They saw him as a loose cannon, among other things. After he retired, they covered up any reports about his old activities."

"So he was a vigilante," said Enigma, piecing it together in his head. "Not an Association-sanctioned hero."

"Neither one of us were," Dick said meaningfully. "After I left to join the Association, Richard retired and went under the radar. We haven't spoken since."

Enigma mulled this over for a moment. "You think Richard may be planning something against the Association now?" he guessed.

"No," Dick answered immediately and quickly. "No, I think Richard wanted to get as far from the Association as he could. I want you to track him down, though. He never told me why he hated the Association so much, but I need to find out why now."

"Hm," said Enigma. "That might actually be easier than tracking down Richard Oakstone himself. If he's gone underground, there won't be much of a trail for me to follow. Especially if what you said about the Association covering up his activities is true."

"It is," Dick insisted.

"I never said I didn't believe you," Enigma told the man. "But you're talking about digging through his past, not looking for him in the present. There are always records left lying around that everybody forgets about. Something in one of those most likely has a clue as to what Oakstone's connection to the Association was. If we go from there, we'll find an answer to your question."

"Okay," Dick said, sighing with relief. "Start there, but I'd still like to talk to Oakstone in person if you could look for him too."

"I'll do my best," Enigma said sincerely. "Chances are, there's a clue or two on where he might have gone in his past records as well."

"Good." Dick paused. "And please be careful. I know how people see the Association, good or bad, but it isn't like how anybody on the outside suspects."

Enigma laughed. "Chill out, buddy," he told the stranger on the phone. "I may be a member, but I'm not stupid."

With that statement, Enigma hung up the phone. Running through the conversation he'd just had for a moment, the trench-coat-clad hero stood up slowly from his chair and stretched. He'd been occupying the same spot for too long, and the stiffness in his body proved it. Furthermore, the mask he wore had become suffocating. Grasping it with both hands, Enigma tore his face away, revealing that of Charlie Quin.

Charlie gasped, able to breathe and feel air on his face at last. Holding Enigma's face in his hands for a moment, he stared at the Chinese kanji of *mi*, meaning secret or confidential. It suited the superhero role he had adopted.

After removing the coat, Charlie undid the sweat-soaked shirt and stood underneath the air-conditioning vent hanging overhead, sighing with relief as it kicked in. The house was hot to him, thanks to his uniform. Once he was cool enough, Charlie stepped out from behind the desk of his office study and walked toward the door.

Before he could turn the knob, a light tapping sounded. Curious, Charlie popped the door open and peeked out. Meredith, his wife of three years, was standing on the other side looking severely irate.

"Can you come out of there for a few minutes?" she demanded, giving him a piercing stare for good measure. "I need your help with something."

Charlie stepped back far enough to open the door the rest of the way so he could step through it. Meredith was watching the whole time, a scowl of disapproval masking her face as the door closed behind him.

"Baxter's upstairs," she stated flatly.

Charlie looked at his wife and blinked. They were almost the same height, so meeting her shrewd eyes wasn't a challenge for him.

"What do you want me to do about it?" he wondered. "I assumed you were the one who invited him here."

Meredith looked taken aback momentarily. "You knew?" she demanded. "You knew he was here this whole time, and you didn't do anything?"

Charlie shrugged, uninterested. "I saw his car pull up across from our house right before I came downstairs. I assumed you had called him back, so I went back to work in my study so you both could have a little privacy."

Meredith's scowl flattened and took on something resembling bemusement. "You mean," she started, having trouble forming whole words. "You don't mind?"

Charlie shrugged again. It was becoming something of a trademark gesture whenever he and his wife conversed, which wasn't happening a whole lot these days.

"You were the one who said you weren't happy being monogamous," Charlie reminded, forcing his voice to stay calm. "I don't like Baxter, and I made myself clear as to why, but you kept inviting him to join us. When I decided to abstain, you said that was fine, but then you told me he was getting possessive."

"He was," Meredith replied, a bit too insistently for Charlie's comfort.

"Then why is he here?" Charlie asked point blank. "Did he break down the door? I would assume no, since I didn't hear a crash or you screaming for help at any point, or police sirens for that matter."

"He didn't break in," Meredith said defensively. "I invited him."

Charlie stared his wife down hard. She had gone on the defensive, something she once would have never done. These days, however, her confidence had been rattled. Charlie knew he had the advantage. A part of him didn't want to take it, but he quickly shushed the nagging voice in his head.

"You invited Baxter in," Charlie began, emphasizing each word forcefully but smoothly. "You invited that man back into our home after ignoring my warnings for months and then saying he wasn't allowed back in this house."

To her credit, whatever that meant at this point, Meredith looked the teensiest bit ashamed.

"Did he go upstairs to our bedroom, or did you invite him?" Charlie pressed.

Meredith didn't answer, which was really all the confirmation Charlie needed. Meredith had never had a reason to feel ashamed before. Baxter had become her weakness, it seemed, and much as Charlie felt like the bad guy in this situation, he had every intention of using that weakness against her.

"Go upstairs," he told his wife flatly.

Meredith's eyes widened. "What?" she wondered.

"You heard me," he barked, letting the anger he felt trickle into his voice now. "Go upstairs. He's waiting for you. You know what Baxter gets like when you don't give him what he wants. It doesn't worry you that you're down here talking to me instead of taking care of his needs right now?"

Meredith took a step back, thinking Charlie was going to lunge at her. However, Charlie was merely turning slightly so he could walk around her.

"Where do you think you're going?" Meredith demanded, once she realized he was walking away.

"To work," he told her, not slowing his pace or looking back over his shoulder. "Someone's got to pay the electric bill this month."

"I already paid it!" Meredith shouted back at him. "Are you leaving me alone in this house with that man?"

Charlie continued on down through the hallway to the foyer past their kitchen, which led to the backyard and their garage. Stopping halfway outside, he turned back and stared at the woman he'd vowed to cherish for the rest of his life.

"You figure it out," he told her coldly, before letting the door slam shut behind him.

THEIR DRIVEWAY circled around to the back of the house. The garage was facing the gazebo near the picket fence, which was where Charlie stored his motorcycle. Meredith had called it his "midlife-crisis vehicle" when he'd brought it home. Charlie had bought the damn thing at his partner's insistence, but Meredith used any excuse she could these days to tease him.

Revving the engine, Charlie let the sensation roll over his body. It helped him forget about what might be going on upstairs in his own house at the moment. With a sigh, he slapped on his helmet and took off, closing the garage door with a push of the button on his steering wheel.

It felt good to be on the road again.

Taking the long way, Charlie raced through the back roads of the community that lurked on the outskirts of town. The woodland area near the coast was pretty, if slightly too upper-middle class for his tastes. Despite being a part of that particular rank, Charlie had never felt at home in it. It was another thing he and his partner shared in common.

The foremost thing being that he and the American Gladiator were both bisexual.

It was the one thing he'd kept secret from Meredith since they'd begun dating. Before that time, he'd wrestled with his orientation and place in the world, supplementing real-life experiences with hours of Internet porn. When Meredith and he had gotten serious, he'd assumed the phase would pass, that it was indeed a phase left over from junior high and nothing more.

Time had proven otherwise, and as things between him and Meredith grew strained, Charlie had found himself falling back on old surfing habits. Meredith had blamed work, Charlie, the neighborhood, Charlie, the Catholic mindset of the Gulf coast in general, and Charlie.

Then the big idea had hit her.

Charlie had known from the beginning that Meredith was no saint, nor was she anything close to resembling a traditional Catholic virgin child. She'd been reading about swinging couples and open marriages. At least, that was the story she'd fed Charlie. Either way, it was something she'd wanted to try. Charlie hated admitting it then, but the idea had merit. He might finally find someone with whom he shared a common interest, sexually.

That idea had fallen flat quick. Most of the men Meredith selected were jerks who thought he was some sort of narrow-eyed weak chink. A couple of them had staggered out the front door afterward limping and breathing unevenly. Meredith hadn't been happy, but to keep her from flying off the handle at him anymore, Charlie had drawn up a charter listing the things he was willing to do from then on, and who with. He also stipulated that he did not always have to be present when Meredith brought a guest over for some fun. It had seemed like the best way to keep her happy during the months when he had a heavy workload.

As Enigma, Charlie specialized in missing persons and runaways. The Association often brought him assignments, most of them dealing with the errant children of wealthy businessmen who resented the hell out of their parents being away so much. To increase his income, Charlie also worked pro bono cases as a tax write-off and took jobs on the side from the slice of labor that weren't part of the wealthy elite.

The job was rough, but nothing compared to the turn his married life had taken.

"It would be fine if you could just meet someone you connected with too."

That had been Meredith's answer each time he'd brought up the idea of them going back to being monogamous, even temporarily.

What she didn't know was that Charlie already had.

Charlie took the turn on the right, rolling up in front of a small but nicely built trailer that had a deck encircling the whole frame. Before he had killed his engine, a figure was stepping outside.

The American Gladiator, Tyrone to his friends, was wearing a huge shit-eating grin on his face as he strolled calmly outside in his boxers, which were printed appropriately enough with the American flag.

"Charlie, boy!" Ty called out happily. "What's your lazy ass doing here? Did the old lady finally toss you out?"

Charlie laughed in spite of himself as he removed his helmet. "Nah," he replied, climbing off the bike. "She still needs someone to pay her half of the bills."

Ty vaulted over the side of the deck onto the grass. As Charlie approached, the giant-sized black man with muscles in places that made Charlie green with envy tossed his arms open wide. Charlie was expecting a hug, but the minute Ty had Charlie in his arms, he placed a big wet kiss on his partner's mouth.

"Come inside," Ty said, once he'd left his best friend breathless. "We gotta finish something you started last time."

Charlie let himself be led up the stairs into Ty's trailer. The place was spotless as always, hardly the picture of a bachelor pad.

"We've got a new case," Charlie managed to get out before Ty was kissing him again.

"Fuck that shit," Ty replied between kisses. "I miss my boy."

Charlie fell silent, surrendering to Ty's expert mouth, and allowed himself to be walked backward down the hall to the American Gladiator's bedroom. There, they stripped each other out of their clothes. Ty took less time to undress for obvious reasons, but Charlie enjoyed having Tyrone's big hands rake over his body.

It had been a few days, too long for either man's peace of mind, so they skipped a lot of the preliminary foreplay and dropped straight into bed between the sheets. Tyrone made a beeline for Charlie's asshole, using his tongue to circle the outer rim in long, slow movements. Charlie, meanwhile, attacked Ty's long shaft with a vengeance.

Charlie couldn't explain why he loved worshiping his partner's manhood so much. There was something hypnotic about the thickness of the shaft, the way it jutted out proudly from the nest of curled hair, accepting all challengers. The taste of its skin was salty, but with an edge of sweetness underneath.

When Ty was ready, Charlie positioned Ty on his back so he could look into his partner's eyes. Shuffling up between the thick trunks that were the American Gladiator's thighs, Charlie mounted him in one deep thrust. The movement made Ty grunt, but he gave no indication of wanting Charlie to stop. Charlie bent forward, continuing his thrusts as he forced his cock in and out of the larger man's body.

Ty was a champion-class kisser, capable of doing things with his mouth that most men couldn't accomplish with half their body. Charlie could feel his toes curl as their tongues wrestled with one another. When Ty raised up suddenly, Charlie pulled away without argument so that Ty could have his turn.

Tyrone loved the doggie-style position. After working together for so long, there was little the two didn't understand about one another. Charlie got on all fours without waiting to be asked and braced himself for invasion. The first part was always the hardest and required a substantial amount of lube. Tyrone kept his asshole lubricated at all times, just in case they had a spare moment to fool around. Charlie wasn't so lucky, always fearing Meredith might discover his secret. In spite of her supposed enlightened view about modern marriage, she'd never had much patience for skipping fences.

Ty knew to take it slow, but Charlie was in no mood to wait. Once his partner was oiled up and had greased his entry point with the tip, Charlie reached around with one hand and seized Ty by the hip, dragging him forward.

"In a hurry today, aren't we?" Ty asked, taking the hint.

"Ump!" Charlie grunted. "Just fuck me, baby. I've waited longer than enough for this."

Ty bent forward once he'd gotten a good rhythm going and placed kisses up and down the back of Charlie's neck, knowing it drove the man underneath him crazy. The two shifted positions more than once, going from on all fours to Charlie riding up and down on Ty's big pole like a starved cowboy.

"Ye-haw," Ty shouted, teasing.

"Bet your ass," Charlie gasped out, impaling himself all the way down, hard.

It was too much for Charlie to take for too long that way. When Ty saw the discomfort begin to spread across Charlie's face, he flipped his partner over onto his back to plow his ass in the missionary position.

"Stop!" Charlie cried out suddenly. "Or I'll go."

Tyrone almost kept going but forced himself to pull out. Getting on his back again, he spread both legs, giving Charlie a good look at the asshole he'd fucked before and would be soon again.

Charlie's eyes softened at the sight. "I love seeing that," he whispered, stroking the inside of Ty's thigh tenderly, lovingly.

"Hurry the fuck up," Ty pleaded, winking his hole at Charlie invitingly. "We can do this ladies' circle bullshit later. I need my boy to plow me good, and I know you need to get your rocks off."

Charlie laughed but did as his partner asked and began ramming his dick in and out again. Ty didn't need much more encouragement. Pretty soon, his dark skin was splotched with white cream that burst out of his cock like a geyser.

"I'm there," Charlie said, seeing his partner go. "I'm right there behind you, baby."

"Don't stop," Ty ordered him. "Keep going, lover. I want to feel you go inside of me this time."

Charlie raised an eyebrow at this but didn't slow his pace. "You sure?" he asked as he felt his balls draw up.

"Hell yeah," said Ty, nodding emphatically. "I've been wantin' this for a while. Put it where it belongs. I want it inside of me."

Charlie increased his speed as he felt his nuts unload. The hot lava of his orgasm flooded into Ty's ass, spilling over the side and staining the sheets. Charlie kept going, the momentum of his orgasm giving him the fuel to keep fucking his partner. Ty grabbed his cock, jerking it like a man possessed and sending another load all over himself again moments later.

The sight was too much for Charlie. His whole body locked up as a dry climax rippled through his muscles. When it faded, he fell forward, right into Ty's arms. His partner was wearing a big grin and a twinkle in his eye as their mouths met.

"I love you, bud," Charlie whispered, fighting to get the words out between the pounding of his heart.

"Always," Ty replied, giving Charlie a warm squeeze. "Always and forever, man."

WHEN CHARLIE awoke, he could hear the television set on in the living room. Glancing at the clock, he saw that it'd only been a few minutes ago when he dozed off.

"Charlie!" Tyrone's voice was thick and panicky, something Charlie wasn't accustomed to hearing. "Get in here."

Opening his eyes wide, Charlie climbed out of bed and threw on the pair of boxers Ty had abandoned on the floor when their lovemaking session had begun.

"What's wrong?" he asked worriedly, coming down the hall from Ty's room to the den area. "What happened?"

The answer was on the television set. Charlie's facial expression went from slack to shocked to horrified before making a full stop at rage.

"What?" he began, trying to form words. "How?"

Ty looked at him with a pained expression, holding himself together, but not by much. "They're saying it happened an hour or so ago," Ty explained. "Just before you got here."

Charlie felt sick. For a moment, he was afraid of throwing up all over Ty's clean carpet. Then he felt Ty's hands on his shoulders, and things steadied somewhat.

"Come here," Ty said, leaving no room for dispute in his voice.

Charlie followed Ty's lead and found himself being placed on one of the stools that lined the countertop separating Ty's den and kitchen areas. Ty milled around for a bit, gathering up two glasses, brandy, and whiskey. Filling each glass with ice first, Ty made the two of them a mixed concoction that flowed between the ice cubes, keeping Charlie distracted.

"Do they know who?" Charlie asked as Ty scooted the drink over to him.

Ty pointed at Charlie's glass insistently before taking a sip of his own. "Not yet," Ty said, watching closely as Charlie sipped his drink, letting the alcohol calm his nerves. "I heard shit about terrorism, of course, both foreign and domestic, but no one has anything concrete right now."

Charlie swiveled his stool around to face the television. On screen, the Association building in Chicago was in flames.

"Can I have another?" Charlie asked, before finishing his drink off in a few gulps.

"Sure," Ty replied. "Looks like we're both gonna need it."

Most of the afternoon passed with them sitting in front of the TV watching news reports and making phone calls. Charlie had wanted to confirm that none of their friends had been at the home base when the attack occurred. A lot of the lines were tied up, but as Ty reminded him, it most likely meant they were doing the same thing.

Luckily, Ty's laptop was booted up, and he'd installed Wi-Fi in the trailer a month ago. Pretty soon, they were getting confirmation e-mails from fellow Association members and staff, letting everyone know who was alive, who was injured, and who had been declared dead.

Charlie finally worked up the nerve to call Meredith, hoping the whole time the phone rang that she wasn't in the middle of something. When Meredith answered, his mind was somewhere between relieved and disgusted.

"Have you been watching the news?" he asked.

Meredith didn't answer right away. "I sent Baxter home," she said instead. "Right after you left. And I told him not to come back anymore. Are you coming home soon?"

Charlie blinked. "Meredith," he began slowly. "The Association headquarters was attacked. They're saying bombs were placed inside of it. I'm at Tyrone's place trying to help people make sense out of all of it."

Most of the remaining conversation was a blur. After reassurances that he was all right, as well as reminders that the headquarters of the Association was located in Chicago, Charlie told Meredith good-bye.

"I need to go," he said. "We're trying to help catalog a database of what everybody knows. It might help with the investigation."

"We need to talk when you get home," Meredith said quickly. "There are some things I think I should tell you."

Charlie froze, then glanced across the couch at Ty, who'd been tapping away furiously at the keyboard on his laptop.

"Me too," he said softly. "I'll call you again later. Bye."

Charlie set his phone down on the coffee table in front of them, staring at it for several minutes and thinking about everything and nothing at the same time.

"Problems on the home front?" Ty inquired.

Charlie shook his head, the sound of Ty's voice snapping him out of his malaise. "Nothing that can't wait," he answered, glancing up. "Would it be all right with you if I spent the night?"

Ty looked up from his laptop. "We don't have to do anything," Charlie added quickly. "Now doesn't really feel like the best time anyway. I just...."

Hesitating, Charlie met Tyrone's eyes. "I'd just rather be here with you," he finished. "I know I'm needed here, and I know we can do some good."

Slowly, he reached across and took Ty's hand in his. "And I want to be here," he confessed. "With you."

Ty's smile was a mixture of sorrow and relief, a testament to the tragedy they were both struggling with.

"Okay by me," he said, giving Charlie's hand a squeeze.

"Good," replied Charlie, scooting across the couch to sit by his partner's side. "Real good."

J.L. O'FAOLAIN was born the youngest, with four older sisters, in the backwoods of the Deep South. Those that have braved getting to know him have attributed this to being the root of his growing insanity. A teased bibliophile in his youth, O'Faolain spent his years prior to getting published as a cook, laundry man, delivery boy, grease monkey, and retail stocker. He has a plethora of skills and abilities, none of which would work well on a job application. In his spare time, O'Faolain enjoys weightlifting, philosophy, deconstruction, reading, writing, porn, and the Internet in general. Aside from becoming a successfully published author, he would very much like to pilot a giant robot while Two-Mix's "Rhythm Emotion" is playing in the background. Either that, or travel the world in a dirigible. In short, the general consensus by all, including himself, is that he is a mighty strange fellow.

Section Thirteen Stories from J.L. O'FAOLAIN

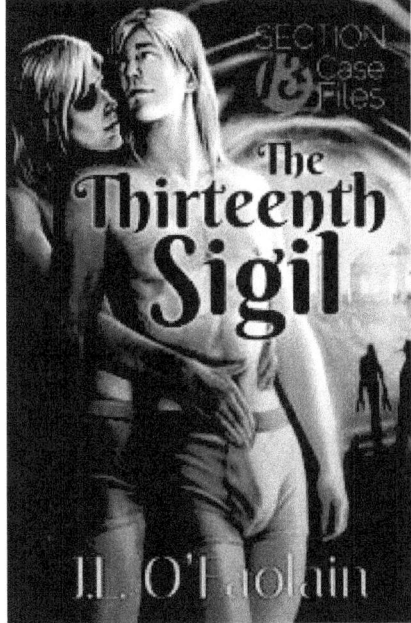 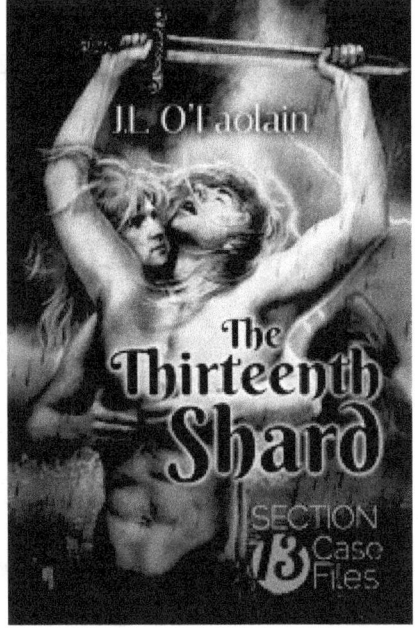

http://www.dreamspinnerpress.com

www.ingramcontent.com/pod-product-compliance
Lightning Source LLC
Chambersburg PA
CBHW060103260626
47160CB00005B/1784